# THE GREAT CARAVAN CATASTROPHE

BY MARK LOWERY

**The Roman Garstang Adventures**

*The Jam Doughnut that Ruined My Life*
*The Chicken Nugget Ambush*
*Attack of the Woolly Jumper*
*The Great Caravan Catastrophe*

# THE GREAT CARAVAN CATASTROPHE

## MARK LOWERY

Piccadilly
PRESS

First published in Great Britain in 2017 by
PICCADILLY PRESS
80–81 Wimpole St, London W1G 9RE
www.piccadillypress.co.uk

A CIP catalogue record for this book
is available from the British Library.

ISBN: 978-1-84812-613-8
also available as an ebook

1

Typeset by Palimpsest Book Production Ltd, Falkirk, Stirlingshire
Printed and bound by Clays Ltd, St Ives Plc

Piccadilly Press is an imprint of Bonnier Zaffre Ltd,
a Bonnier Publishing company
www.bonnierpublishing.com

To Sar, Jam, Sam and The Googliser

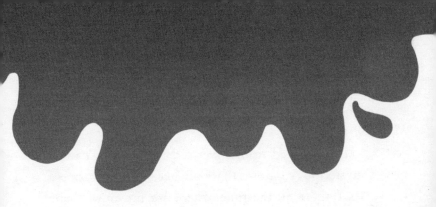

My name's Roman Garstang. There are loads of things that I'm *pretty sure* I'll never do, like:

- Wear someone else's underpants.
- Give up doughnuts again.
- Milk a giraffe.
- Train a squid to tap-dance.
- Trim my toenails with a chainsaw.
- Eat a salad.

But there's one thing I'm absolutely, definitely, one hundred per cent certain I will never do. **Ever.** I swear on the grave of the school stick insect, Timmy the Twiglet (RIP).

I will **NEVER** get married.

Mum says I'm too young to think this and it'll all change when I 'discover girls'.

Rubbish.

I don't need to *discover* girls. They aren't rare, mysterious creatures that only live under volcanoes. I see them all the time. There are fifteen of them in my class.

Plus, I *like* girls. In fact, fifty per cent of my friends are girls. OK, so that actually only equals **one** girl (Vanya Goyal), but she's definitely the better half of my friends. The other half is called Darren Gamble. He's the craziest kid on the planet. Last week he swallowed a battery, 'to see what would happen'.

He had to go to hospital, in case you were wondering.

Nope. It's got nothing to do with girls. I just don't want to have a wedding. I *hate* weddings. Up until last month I'd been to two in my whole life and they were both awful.

Weirdly, everyone else thinks weddings are brilliant. Nobody but me can see how terrible they are. How can people not realise? The biggest clue is that people *cry* at them.

Normal people only cry when things are sad or

painful. The last time I cried was because something was sad *and* painful. It was last Tuesday at Timmy the Twiglet's funeral, when Darren Gamble sneaked up behind me and gave me a 'turbo-powered double-nuclear purple-nurple nipple-twister'.

By the way, Timmy the Twiglet's painful death was all Gamble's fault. He'd mistaken the poor thing for a real stick and had tried to make a fire by rubbing him together with another twig.

I told you: the kid's deranged.

It's a fact: weddings are grim. Silly clothes, even sillier hats, grown-ups dancing like electrocuted baboons. Even wedding *cake* is rubbish. You won't believe this if you've never been to one, but they only serve fruit cake.

I'm not even joking. As in **cake** with **fruit** in it! Cakes aren't meant to be healthy! Has the world gone mad? What kind of sicko thought of that? And what will they come up with next? Cabbage-flavoured doughnuts? Sprout crumble? A Twix made out of celery and liquidised prunes?

But it gets worse.

At your wedding you've actually got to *kiss* your wife. In front of everyone. Including your mum. **Gross!**

This would be the most embarrassing thing of all time, but even *that's* not all. Kissing's meant to be romantic but it's actually deadly. When you kiss someone, you swap about eighty million bacteria between your mouths!

*Eighty million!*

That's more germs than there are people in the whole of Britain! Every time you pucker up for a snog, you're risking your life. You'd be better off coughing in each other's faces, or even licking your toilet bowl. Nobody thinks *those* things are romantic, though, do they? People don't cheer and take photos of you if you shove your face down the bog and start slurping away with your tongue.

In fact, when Gamble did it in the school loos, our teacher Mrs McDonald called him a dirty beast and made him wash his mouth out with soapy water.

So I've always thought that weddings were awful. Then, last week, I went to one that made me change my mind. I don't think that weddings are awful any more.

Now I think they're absolutely *evil*.

People on TV are forever banging on about their *dream* wedding. For me, a dream wedding wouldn't be a good thing because recently I've been having a lot of weird dreams. In them, I'm a massive jam doughnut being chased by angry chicken nuggets that are dressed in horrible woolly jumpers.

Imagine *that* kind of dream wedding. It'd almost be as bad as the real one I went to.

# MONDAY

# One Week Before the Wedding

## Awful Plans are Made and I Get a Date

I first learned I was going to a wedding a few Mondays ago, exactly one week before it took place. Most people find out about weddings months ahead, when they receive a pretty invitation in the post.

The way I found out wasn't as pleasant.

I was minding my own business on the playground before school, enjoying my post-breakfast doughnut. Then Rosie Taylor – the worst human who's ever lived – suddenly appeared from nowhere and shoved her face into mine. 'Why are you ruining my life again, you puke-tastic little skidmark?'

Told you she's nasty.

I nearly dropped my doughnut. 'What have I done now?'

Rosie blames me for everything that goes wrong in her life, even if it's nothing to do with me. Seriously, she once tried to get me chucked out of school because she found a fly in her lunch. She said this was *my* fault because I'm 'so smelly that flies follow me in a swarm' and I should be expelled because I'm a 'public health risk'.

Rosie jabbed her finger into my chest. 'I've just found out that your cousin Lee is marrying my cousin Kat next Monday. How can *you* be in the same family as *me*? You're barely in the same species.'

I couldn't reply to this because I had a lot to get my head round all at once:

1) I wasn't expecting to see Rosie. She hadn't been at school for a whole week since sneezing all over Princess Lucy (the future queen) during a royal visit to the town. This is a long story involving a flying badger. Rosie had been hiding out at her

family's holiday home in Barbados ever since then because the sneeze had made her world famous.

2) I already knew that my cousin Lee was marrying a girl called Kat. But I had no idea that Kat was related to Rosie Taylor. For a start, she seemed quite nice. And I've already mentioned that Rosie Taylor is definitely not nice. A few days earlier, a parcel from Barbados had arrived at my house. Inside it was a rotting dead octopus and a note from Rosie that said: 'I've finally found something even uglier than you. It's got a nicer personality, though, and it smells much better. Maybe it could take your place at school before I get back.' She doesn't like me very much.

3) While I was dealing with these two surprises, Rosie was still jabbering away, and it was hard to think straight.

'. . . and your cousin must be as nasty as you because *I* wasn't even invited.'

I could definitely understand why Lee and Kat hadn't invited Rosie to the wedding. I wouldn't invite her to anything. She once ruined this girl called Chloe's birthday by telling Chloe's mum that the party was a 'tacky mess' and she'd have had more fun at home, 'scraping dead skin off my verrucas'.

'How could they have a wedding without *hashtag Rosie Taylor* there?' Rosie continued, the lips of her little slug's bum mouth tight and pale. 'Obviously, Kat was worried that I'm so gorgeous that I'd make her look like a flagly little troll.'

'Flagly?' I asked.

Rosie tutted. 'Flabby and ugly, you cheese-brained moron.'

Rosie thinks she's beautiful, but actually she's got a face like a smashed piano. I swallowed a mouthful of doughnut and changed the subject. 'I thought you were in Barbados.'

She sighed, like it was hard work talking to someone as dumb as me. 'The thought of my cousin marrying into your family makes me feel like stabbing myself in the head with a fork. But my mum and I were so angry about being snubbed that we flew straight back here. As soon as I landed, I stormed round to see Kat and Lee, and demanded an invite or I would find an old gypsy woman to curse their unborn children.'

'Normal reaction,' I said. *Well, for Rosie, anyway.*

Rosie narrowed her eyes at me. 'So obvs Kat said

I could come. But then your idiot cousin Lee said that if *my* family was coming then *your* family should come too.'

'You mean . . . ?'

'Yes,' snapped Rosie. 'You and your dismal parents are going to get an invite as well, which is going to ruin everything. They might as well invite a gang of chimpanzees. The chimps have better table manners for a start. And, unlike the Garstangs, they can be trained not to poo in their hands and fling it at the walls.'

I ignored the insult because this was serious.

I didn't want to go to the wedding. I'd been relieved when Lee had told us he was sorry but they didn't have space to invite everyone so we weren't going to be able to come. But now, thanks to Rosie, I was going to have to wear a tie and sit through all the stupid speeches and dances and kisses. Not to mention the depressing fruit cake.

But things were about to get a lot worse.

'And do you know where they're getting married?' asked Rosie.

I licked a blob of jam off my finger and shook my head. Maybe my cousin Lee had told us once but I wouldn't have been listening. There's only one thing more boring than *being* at a wedding and that's *talking* about a wedding. I'd rather be savaged by wild hamsters than sit through a wedding chat.

Rosie tutted. 'Like, hundreds of miles away in the middle of a field on some mingtastic farm.'

'Is that bad?'

'Course it is, you dribbling crud spoon.'

*Crud spoon?* Whatever that was, it didn't sound nice.

'My mum said we should travel down there with your family and "make a weekend of it".'

She said this like it was the worst thing in the world.

Which of course it was.

My belly felt like it was falling out. 'What?'

'You heard,' she growled. 'We're going on holiday together.'

Then she pulled the remainder of the doughnut out of my hand, dropped it to the ground and crushed it under her high heel.

# TUESDAY

# Evening

## The Taylors Take Charge of the Wedding

'Oooh, it's lovely!' cooed Mum, as we pulled into the gravel driveway outside Rosie's house. 'Now remember, Roman. Best behaviour. We're mixing with rich people tonight.'

Rosie's parents had invited us round to plan our weekend away together. This was not my idea of fun. In fact, I'd have rather spent the evening being puked on by this kid in my class called Kevin Harrison, who throws up so often his nickname is Ali Blargh Blargh and the Forty Heaves.

Huffing out my cheeks, I climbed out of the car and looked around. Rosie's house is *massive*. It's built out of huge grey stones so it looks like a castle, complete with turrets on the roof and floodlights so it stands out at night. The back garden is the size of four football pitches. Rosie's pony used to live there (until Rosie fell off it and had it sent to China to work in a nuclear waste dump as punishment).

Rosie's dad owns a great big shopping centre in town, and she never shuts up about how much money her family has. This doesn't make them nice people though. I've already said that Rosie is probably the nastiest person in the universe. Her mum is just a grown-up version of her – loud, vain and rude – and her dad's a cruel bighead. One time Rosie boasted that he sacked a woman from his shopping centre for being 'so butt-ugly she was scaring the customers away'.

In fact, I was amazed that the Taylors had asked us to come with them at all. Rosie once told me that her mum comes out in a rash if she goes near a poor person. And Rosie's mum's idea of a poor person is someone who only owns three houses.

But I had bigger things to worry about, like how I was going to get through four whole days with Rosie without wanting to eat my own brain.

'Do we have to do this?' whined Dad, as we

crunched our way up to the front door. He was almost as unhappy about this weekend as I was.

'Be nice,' said Mum. 'They're going to be family now.'

I said nothing. Frankly, I'd prefer to be related to Darren Gamble's dog's bum worms than to Rosie and her parents.

'And just think,' continued Mum, her eyes misting over, 'if we all get on well, this could be the first of many holidays together. They might invite us out to their villa in Barbados, or their ski chalet in Switzerland.'

Dad and I looked at each other, horrified. I couldn't think of anything worse.

There was a huge sign by the front door that read:

# TAYLOR TOWERS – OUR DOGS ARE TRAINED TO ATTACK CHARITY COLLECTORS

*How lovely,* I thought.

Mum rang the bell and, a few moments later, Rosie's mum opened the door. She was dressed like a glamorous movie star – flowing white dress and huge sunglasses (even though she was indoors and it was dark outside) – and she was dripping with jewellery. 'Oh, hello!' she gushed, kissing my mum on both cheeks. 'I love your skirt. It's *fabulous*!'

Mum blushed. 'It's nothing really. I bought it at the supermarket.'

Mrs Taylor's face dropped. 'A supermarket?' she said, as if Mum had just told her she'd stolen it off a dead person. 'You mean one of those shops where people buy cat food and toilet tissue?'

Mum nodded awkwardly.

Then, for some reason, Rosie's mum suddenly burst out laughing. 'Classic!' she howled, snorting like an asthmatic walrus. 'You had me going there. I almost believed you. Only a complete peasant would buy clothes at a supermarket.'

'But I *did* get it from a supermarket,' said Mum, confused.

Rosie's mum stopped laughing. 'Oh. Poor you.'

Mum didn't know what to say.

'Don't worry,' said Rosie's mum. 'One weekend with me and I'll have you looking a million dollars!'

This cheered Mum up immediately. 'That sounds exciting.'

'And expensive,' grumbled Dad. He doesn't like spending money.

'You must see the new indoor swimming pool!' sang Rosie's mum, leading my mum off into the house.

Dad and I trooped inside after her and . . . *oh my word*! It was humungous! The hallway was as big as a church, with a marble staircase sweeping up to the first floor. For a moment, I was seriously impressed.

Then I saw it.

Hanging on the wall was the creepiest thing I've ever seen – a framed oil painting of Rosie, dressed as a princess in a glittery dress and a gold crown. It was about three times as big as me, and the glaring eyes seemed to follow me around.

'Good grief!' I said.

'Beautiful, isn't she?' said Rosie's dad, appearing from nowhere.

I said nothing. 'Beautiful' wasn't the word I'd use to describe the picture. 'Terrifying' was more like it. I was pretty sure I'd be having nightmares for the rest of my life.

He slapped my dad on the shoulder. 'Incredible house, eh?'

'I like the turrets,' said Dad, even though I guessed he didn't.

Rosie's dad laughed. 'We like to hide behind them and pour boiling oil onto any poor people who come round begging for money. Ha!' With that he gave Dad an even bigger slap on the shoulder, which caused him to stagger forward a few paces. 'And this must be Brogan.'

I realised he was talking to me. 'It's Roman. And actually I've met you bef—'

'Funny . . .' he interrupted, peering closely at my face. 'Rosie said you look like a bug-eyed lizard with a skin disease.'

*That was nice of her*, I thought.

'Can't see it myself,' he continued, straightening himself up. 'To me you look fairly normal.'

*Thanks a bunch.* Maybe one day I'll have that put on my gravestone:

### HERE LIES ROMAN GARSTANG. HE LOOKED FAIRLY NORMAL.

At this point, Mum came back from the kitchen with Mrs Taylor, looking as if she'd just seen a doughnut the size of Saturn. 'It's like a palace!'

'It is, isn't it?' smarmed Rosie's mum.

'So,' said Rosie's dad, 'looking forward to the weekend? Three nights away with us? You must be thrilled.'

'Can't wait,' we all said together. Mum said it enthusiastically enough to drown out Dad and me. We both sounded pretty down about it.

Rosie's mum didn't notice. 'Come through. We're about to video-call Lee and Kat about the wedding.'

We followed her into the living room. I felt relieved to escape from the portrait of Rosie. But this didn't last long because I found the real thing sitting in the middle of a white leather sofa, opposite a massive TV.

But then something *really* weird happened.

'OMG!' cried Rosie, leaping to her feet, 'How fabalicious to see you, Mrs Garstang! Hashtag: welcome to Taylor Towers!'

She skipped over to Mum with a big smile on her face and gave her a hug. *A hug!* I was so shocked I nearly fell over.

Rosie Taylor was being NICE!

This had literally never happened before. I'd have been less surprised if she'd turned into a frog and farted 'We Wish You a Merry Christmas' through a flute.

'Please sit down,' said Rosie. 'There are a few things that Lee and Kat might want to change about their wedding.'

I frowned. *They* might want to change? It sounded a bit fishy to me.

She pulled out a wireless keyboard and tapped away on it. A symbol of a ringing telephone appeared on the TV.

After a few rings, my cousin Lee and his fiancée Kat appeared onscreen. They were holding hands on a sofa. 'Hi, everyone!'

We all said hi back.

'Uncle Tony,' said Kat to Rosie's dad, 'we can't believe you've offered to pay for our whole wedding!'

'So kind!' said Lee. 'You shouldn't have.'

Mum, Dad and I turned to Rosie's dad, mouths open.

'Mnya,' he said, 'bit of loose change.'

*Loose change?*

I only know two things about weddings: 1) They're totally awful; and 2) They're totally expensive.

Why had Rosie's dad offered to pay?

'OK, business time,' said Rosie. 'We're all still furious that you didn't invite us to the wedding straight away.'

Rosie's mum smiled at us. 'Isn't it wonderful that she's so confident?'

*Confident?* I'd probably have said 'rude'.

Onscreen, Lee tried to smile. 'Sorry. Numbers were tight. You're coming now though. We found space.'

'*Found space?* For me?' snapped Rosie. 'I'm hashtag Rosie Taylor, not an old sofa. Anyway, you'll be pleased to know we've decided not to take revenge.'

*Revenge!* I thought. *Wow!*

'Oh. Er. Thanks,' said Kat.

Rosie gave her sweetest smile, which made her look like an evil doll that had just come to life and was about to murder someone. 'Instead, we're going to ask you to make a few teeny-weeny changes to your plans.'

Kat looked confused. 'What do you mean?'

And then it all made sense: Rosie's dad was going to *pay* for the wedding so that Rosie could *control* it.

Rosie flicked her hair back. 'If you own a

gorgeous car, you don't keep it in the garage, do you? So if you've got a gorgeous guest at the wedding, you don't tuck her away on the back row. I'll obviously be chief bridesmaid.'

'I've already got a ch—' began Kat, but Rosie talked over her.

'And I'll be in charge of carrying the wedding rings. And meeting the guests when they arrive. And you'll probably want me to sing when you're walking down the aisle. I've been told I have a voice like a songbird.'

I shouldn't have laughed here but I couldn't help myself. A *songbird*?! When Rosie sings, she sounds more like an ostrich being kicked to death.

Rosie pretended she hadn't heard me. 'Have you got a priest to do the ceremony?'

'Well – there's a lady coming from the registry office...' said Lee, looking shell-shocked.

Rosie sniffed. 'Hmm. It's too late for me to train to do that anyway. I'll let you keep her.'

'Kind of you,' said Kat.

'And I hear you've gone for white flowers,' said Rosie, ignoring the sarcasm. 'Ditch them. They make me look ill. You'll need pink ones to highlight my natural glow.'

I suppose Rosie does have a natural glow about her. Like a Halloween lantern.

'And tell the photographer that he is strictly forbidden from taking photos from my right because that's my least beautiful side.'

Lee cleared his throat. 'You know, it *is* a bit late for all these changes . . .'

'You'd better work fast then,' replied Rosie. 'I expect a daily email to tell me what you've done.'

'But . . .'

Rosie took a deep breath. 'Ever since I sneezed on that princess I've been all over the internet. The whole world has either been laughing at me or calling me names. So I need to come out fighting. I need to show everyone that Rosie Taylor is on her way back. And your wedding is the perfect chance for me to do this. My first public appearance since the Princess Incident. Oh, and I'll be bringing a guest.'

'But we told you,' whined Lee, 'numbers are tight.'

'Then *un-invite* someone,' Rosie said, as though this was completely obvious. 'There must be someone old or rubbish or smelly on the guest list. Defriend them. Liquidise them. For all I care you can cover them in peanut butter and feed them to a man-eating squirrel. I need to have someone who can film me for my new internet channel.'

'Internet channel?' I asked.

Rosie barely looked at me. 'Rosie-dot-TV. I launched it last week. It brings all my social media together in one place. Now my fans only have to go to one website to watch me.'

'What a great idea!' said Mum.

*Eh?* A Rosie-based TV channel was the worst idea since lemon-curd doughnuts. Who on earth would watch Rosie on the internet? Well, apart from drooling idiots, of course.

'Thanks, Mrs Garstang. I've already got seventy thousand subscribers,' simpered Rosie, before turning angrily back to the screen. 'The whole point of you two getting married is to give people the chance to see me at the wedding.'

'I thought the point of us getting married was that we love each other,' said Kat, who sounded close to tears.

Rosie rolled her eyes. 'Whatever. Just remember who's paying.'

Lee sighed. 'We'll see what we can do.'

'No. You'll do it.'

Rosie hung up before he could reply. 'That went fabtastically well,' she said, wriggling about excitedly. 'Now. I must go and plan. Plus I've got to film myself brushing my hair before bed, otherwise the internet will literally shut down. Toodles!'

With that, she skipped out of the room and up the stairs.

'Rosie's amazing!' exclaimed Mum. 'She knows what she wants and she just goes and gets it.'

My jaw nearly fell off. *Amazing?* Had Mum gone mental?

Rosie's dad grinned. 'That's my girl! Taught her everything she knows. Big lesson for you there, Wogan.'

'Roman,' I said flatly.

'Whatever,' he replied. 'You've gotta take charge. Otherwise people tell you what to do.'

'But isn't it *Lee and Kat's* wedding?' I said.

Rosie's dad burst out laughing. '*Was* their wedding.'

'But now the Taylors are coming,' added her mum. 'And we do things our way.'

'Oh,' I said.

'Right, well, you're going to have to leave. I've got a motorhome salesman coming round in ten minutes,' said Rosie's dad, practically shoving us towards the door.

'New motorhome?' asked Mum keenly.

'Thought we'd treat ourselves for the holiday,' said Rosie's mum. 'What will you be staying in?'

Dad scratched his neck. 'Well, we've got this old caravan . . .'

'*Old?*' said Rosie's dad, like he meant 'diseased'. 'You don't want to sleep in a tatty old thing. People will think you're a bunch of tramps.'

Mum suddenly looked worried.

Rosie's mum tapped Dad playfully on the hand. 'Go on. Splash out on a new one. This is a special holiday. You're going away with *us* after all.'

Dad tried to smile.

Mum sighed dreamily and leaned right in to Dad's ear. 'What a wonderful family,' she said, just loud enough that I could hear. 'And isn't Rosie *charming?*'

I said nothing. At that exact moment, I happened to be picking my nose. And the gunk under my fingernail was at least a hundred times more charming than Rosie Taylor.

# WEDNESDAY

# Cling-Zillas

The next day, Rosie was back to her normal, nasty self. As I walked through the school gates, she hit me over the head with a brown envelope then thrust it into my hands.

I tried to open it but Rosie slapped my wrist. 'It's not for you. It's for your parents. Anyway, I doubt you'd be able to read it – some of the words have more than three letters.'

Rosie's convinced I'm thick, even though she's not exactly Brain of Britain herself. I mean, she knows everything about clothes and celebrities, but she doesn't know anything about important stuff, like maths or geography or doughnuts.

'If you must know,' she said, 'it's a timetable for the holiday. It tells your dreadful parents where they've got to be for the whole weekend, from the moment we leave on Friday till the wedding on Monday.'

'Why do they have to know that?'

'Because I've got things I need to do and your parents are too thick to organise their own lives.'

I didn't reply. Rosie was making me nervous.

I mean, she'd been sucking up to my mum yesterday, and now she was being horrible about her again. What was she planning? Rosie is never nice to anyone unless she's going to get something out of it. Like the time she wrote that lovely, sweet letter to the local hospital, asking if they'd like to use my body for medical experiments.

'I owe it to my fans to make this trip perfect,' she said, flicking back her hair. 'Rosie-dot-TV is *THE* most important thing in their lives.'

*Wow!* Imagine how rubbish the rest of their lives must be!

'Oh, and BTW, Kat emailed me. Thankfully they've followed my orders and ditched some cling-zillas from the wedding list.'

'Cling-zillas?'

She tutted. 'You know, some ancient great-auntie and an uncle with bad breath. We're each allowed a friend to come with us.'

'Brilliant,' I said. I might have someone other than Rosie to talk to.

'I am, aren't I? At least if you've got a friend you won't be stuck to me all weekend like a lump of dry snot. Just don't bring some vile little slop-bucket who'll ruin everything.'

As she said this, she was looking over at my sort-of mate Darren Gamble, who was rooting through a bin. He pulled out a discarded Dairy Milk wrapper then licked the leftover chocolate off it.

Rosie didn't need to worry about Gamble though. Of course I wouldn't invite *him*. I knew exactly who I'd choose to come with me.

Unfortunately though, and not for the last time, things didn't go to plan.

## My Date

'I'd love to come,' said Vanya Goyal five minutes later. 'But I can't.'

Overhearing, Rosie Taylor cackled at me. I

looked at her sharply and she trotted off. She loves it when bad things happen to me.

I turned back to Vanya. 'Why not?'

She scratched her chin. 'I've got a . . . er . . . karate competition.'

I was going to ask if she could give the competition a miss when Darren Gamble appeared from the toilets, wiping his hands on his trousers. 'What you talking about?'

'Nothing,' I said, as Vanya slinked away.

I didn't want to mention anything to Darren. He might be my friend but I'd never take him to a wedding. He's got terrible manners. One time he told me that he'd been kicked out of a christening for doing a wee in the font.

His little bald, baked-bean-shaped head twitched. 'Rubbish. I heard you inviting what's-her-chops to a wedding, innit.'

I cleared my throat. 'Did I?'

'I'll come,' he said firmly. 'I love weddings, me. I went to *my* cousin's wedding last year and there was a proper good fight afterwards.'

'Oh . . .'

'My grandma headbutted the vicar. It was brutal.'

I didn't have anything to say to this, which was

a shame because it gave Gamble a silence to fill. 'Nice one. Looks like I'm your date then.'

'D-does it?'

'Yep, and you can't go back on it cos you're my bestest mate in the whole world and I love you and if you don't let me come I'll cry for weeks.' He paused to sniff. 'And after I stop crying I'll probably beat you up.'

I gulped.

'This is gonna be well good!' He grinned. Then he celebrated by giving me a wedgie so powerful I thought my eyes were going to pop out.

I was bringing a cling-zilla of my own.

# FRIDAY

# Morning

### The Start of the Horrible Holiday.
### We Get a Caravan Downgrade
### and I Lose Half My Friends

Dad inspected the brand new caravan, which Mum had ordered without telling him. It had been delivered that morning and was now attached to the back of the car.

The caravan was long, sleek and white, and its name – HolidayMaster 3000 – was printed along the side.

'I still don't know what was wrong with our old caravan,' grumbled Dad. 'This must've cost a fortune.'

Mum sighed. 'We're spending the weekend with the *Taylors*. They're like the Royal Family. But richer. We want them to think we're good enough to be their friends, don't we?'

Dad stuck out his bottom lip like a moody toddler. 'I don't want to be friends with them. They're rude show-offs, and I've got a massive bruise on my arm where he keeps whacking me.'

'Be nice,' warned Mum. 'They'll be here in five minutes.'

To me, this weekend sounded more like a prison sentence than a holiday. The only good thing was that Rosie's dad had bullied Mr Noblet, the head teacher, into letting us have three days off school. But then again, since the worst thing about school is spending time with Rosie, I hadn't actually gained anything.

Dad wasn't impressed either. He grunted to himself as he packed the bags into the back of the car.

I had a peek inside the caravan, which I've got to say was pretty awesome. It was really modern and smart. There was a comfy-looking fitted sofa that would fold out to make a bed for Mum and Dad, and a separate twin bedroom for me and Gamble.

*Ah yes.* Gamble.

There was a problem with him.

OK, so there are *loads* of problems with him – the filth, the violence, the way he keeps breaking the law, etc. But on *this* day there was one problem that was bigger than all the others.

I hadn't *exactly* told my parents he was coming.

And at that moment, without knocking, he clomped into the caravan, swigging on a can of Coke. He finished it, smashed it flat against his forehead, then wetly burped the words, 'All right, Roman?' at me.

*Lovely.*

He was carrying a plastic bag in his hand. 'What's in there?' I asked.

'Fireworks!' He grinned. 'Make the wedding go with a bang.'

Gamble and explosives aren't a good combination. One time he brought a homemade bomb to school in his rucksack and the army had to come and detonate it.

He waggled the bag about. 'Don't worry. I'll find somewhere safe to keep 'em.'

'Roman,' hissed Mum from the door. 'A word.'

I stepped out of the caravan. Mum shut the door behind us, sending Dad in to keep watch over Gamble.

'What is *Darren* doing here?' she asked.

'I *was* going to tell you . . .' I said awkwardly.

'Tell me *what*?'

'Gamble is kind of . . . my guest for the weekend.'

Mum looked at me like I'd told her my guest was a flesh-eating zombie. Although the zombie would probably be less dangerous. And it'd definitely smell better.

'Families as posh as the *Taylors* can't spend time with . . . people like Darren,' said Mum.

'There was nobody else,' I said. 'It's not like I could bring Kevin *Ali Blargh Blargh* Harrison, is it? He can't even *look* at a car without throwing up. We'd have been drowning in puke before the end of the drive.'

'I'll call his mum and tell her to come and get him,' said Mum, dialling his house on her mobile. We have the number because Gamble often rings us up just to break wind down the phone.

'Hello, is that Darren's mum?' she said. Someone spoke at the other end, then Mum replied. 'Yes, it is . . . No. I'm afraid we won't be able to take Darren with us to the wedding after all.'

For a few seconds, Mum listened to Mrs Gamble. Her face slowly turned white and her eyes opened wide. Then she ended the call and put the phone back in her handbag.

'I think she *really* wants Darren out of the house for the weekend,' Mum said, her voice shaky. 'She said if we brought him back today she'd be a bit cross.'

'Cross?'

'Well, her exact words were: "If I see that little ratbag before Tuesday, someone might lose an eye."'

'Oh,' I said.

'We'll just have to keep him away from the Taylors and make sure he's on his best behaviour,' said Mum, trying to smile.

*Good luck with that*, I thought. Gamble's idea of best behaviour is saying 'excuse me' before he shoves your finger into an electric pencil sharpener and switches it on.

We went back inside to find him in the middle of the room. Dad was standing in front of him, on his tiptoes with hands outstretched, like a goalkeeper about to face a penalty. His eyes were fixed on Gamble's bag of fireworks.

Gamble drop-kicked his flattened can across the lounge and sat down with his muddy boots up on the sofa. 'You should've told me you wanted a caravan. I could've got you a deal.'

'Feet down, please,' said Dad, anxiously mopping up the Coke drips. 'If I'm going to own a caravan I can't afford, then we can at least keep it clean.'

Gamble put his feet down and wiped them on the carpet. Mum and Dad looked like they might cry.

But things were about to get worse.

There was a scuffling of claws behind us and Gamble's dog, Scratchy, bounded inside. Scratchy is perhaps Europe's most disgusting animal (even worse than Gamble). As well as a serious case of worms, it has patchy fur, fleas, a milky eye and breath that can burn through paint. After a few excited circuits of the lounge, it shuffled along the floor, dragging its bum behind it.

'Get that beast out of here!' screamed Mum.

'Relax,' said Gamble, 'it's the . . .'

'Worms. We know,' I said, as the dog stopped to lick its backside.

Then Gamble did something really vile, even by his standards. He put down the bag of fireworks and gave Scratchy a massive slobbery kiss.

*Horrible*. The dog's tongue had gone from its

worm-infested backside to slopping around Gamble's face in less than two seconds.

'That is the grossest thing I've ever seen,' I said. And when you think that I've known Gamble for several months, this was really saying something. We're talking about a kid who keeps a stack of flattened roadkill toads (or 'toad kill' as he calls them) in his school lunch box alongside his sandwiches.

'So where are me and Scratchy staying, then?' asked Gamble.

'I'm not having that mutt in here,' said Mum.

'Aw!' whined Gamble. 'He'll behave. He's hardly destroyed anything recently.' He scratched a zit on his bald scalp. 'Well. Apart from that person's flower bed. And Dad's armchair. Oh. And that postman.'

I slapped my forehead. *How do you destroy a postman?*

'And you'll have to get rid of the fireworks too,' said Dad.

Gamble tutted. 'I'll find somewhere safe for 'em, innit.'

Just then a car horn sounded on the street and we all looked out of the window. My mouth dropped open. 'Holy doughnuts.'

'Oh, wow,' sighed Mum.

'Forget this pile of junk!' cried Gamble, pointing a bony finger. 'We're staying in THAT!'

## Mansion on Wheels

Dad and I were the first ones outside because Mum nipped to the caravan loo to check her hair. The whole street was blocked by a motorhome. No, more like a full-sized *coach*. It was gleaming and silver with blacked-out windows and a satellite dish on the roof. The driver's door hissed and slid open like something out of *Star Wars*, and Rosie Taylor's mum and dad strutted out, followed by Rosie.

Then I gasped.

Because, after Rosie, out stepped Vanya Goyal: my so-called best friend.

'What are *you* doing here?' I said.

Vanya bit her lip nervously. 'I can explain.'

I felt like I'd been kicked in the guts. 'What about the karate competition?'

'Yeah. About that . . .' Her voice tailed off.

This was awful!

She was meant to be my friend, and she's always

hated Rosie as much as I do. But now she was going on holiday with her behind my back. Or right in front of my face. And now I had to share a caravan with Gamble. 'You . . . lied to me.'

'It's not what you thi—'

'Face it,' interrupted Rosie, 'Vanya's fed up with hanging around with a little butt-comb like you.'

'What's a *butt-comb*?' I asked.

'Google it,' said Rosie, linking arms with Vanya and leading her away. 'Or just look in the mirror.'

Vanya mouthed 'sorry' at me over her shoulder but it was too late. I felt totally crushed.

'Amazing motorhome, eh?' said Rosie's dad, slapping my dad on the shoulder again. 'We call it *Truck*ingham Palace.'

Dad forced a smile at the lame joke and Mr Taylor slapped him once more. The constant slapping seemed like it would get pretty annoying after a while. 'She's basically a luxury mansion on wheels,' Mr Taylor went on. 'When the salesman came round I said, "Just give me the best one you've got, whatever it costs." Only six hundred thousand quid. Bargain eh?'

*Six hundred thousand pounds!* I let this sink in for a moment. That's like . . . hang on . . . er . . .

ten for six pounds . . . so times that by . . . a hundred thousand and you get . . . *NO WAY*!!!

It cost the same as *A MILLION* Squidgy Splodge doughnuts.

I mean, it *was* a pretty sweet motorhome, but come on! *Nothing* could possibly be worth that many doughnuts: they'd last me for at least a week.

Mum joined us out on the street. She glanced from the motorhome to our caravan, which looked pathetic in comparison. 'It's incredible,' she croaked.

'You should see inside,' said Rosie's mum, and pulled her up through the *Star Wars* door.

Rosie tottered back over on her high heels, dragging Vanya behind her. 'When I found out we were staying in a motorhome, I was like: "Seriously – shoot me now. Rosie Taylor does not do camping." But then Daddy rocked up in this mean machine and I was like: "O-M-G! It's beaut-alicious!" That Italian singer Loretta Gobbo has one just for driving from her bedroom to the kitchen.'

Vanya said, 'Wow!' like this was the most amazing thing she'd ever heard.

I glared at her. 'Fascinating.'

Vanya refused to look at me.

'Check this out . . .' said Rosie's dad, leading us

round to the other side. 'Open up!' he commanded. At first I wondered who he was talking to, but then a door on the back of the coach rolled up to reveal a small garage. Inside the garage was a four-seater open-top sports car.

Seriously. There was a flipping sports car in the flipping boot! My flipping eyes nearly popped out of my flipping skull.

'It rolls out so you can dri—'

'Ahem!'

An old woman on a mobility scooter was behind us in the middle of the street. 'You're blocking the road. I can't get past.'

Rosie's dad looked at her like she was a dead fish he'd found behind a radiator. 'Tough luck, you miserable old biddy. I was here first. '

'But I've got to get to the chemist. I've run out of tablets for my heart.'

'You *could* move if . . .' began Dad, but Rosie's dad spoke over him.

'No way. She can go back that way and down the dual carriageway.'

'The *dual carriageway*?' exclaimed Dad. 'But the cars do seventy along there.'

'I'll be squished,' said the old woman.

'Nonsense,' scoffed Rosie's dad. 'You'll probably live.'

'*Probably?*' I said.

'I might not if I don't get to the chemist soon,' she said.

'Better hurry up then,' said Rosie's dad, who actually seemed annoyed with her. 'Survival of the fittest. Chop-chop.'

Mumbling under her breath, the old lady turned her mobility scooter round. As she trundled away, she made an extremely rude hand signal at Rosie's dad's back.

Rosie's dad shook his head. 'What a horrible old woman.'

Dad and I stared at him, speechless, but Rosie didn't seem to think there was anything wrong with his behaviour. She pointed a pink fake nail towards our caravan. 'OMG. What is *that* tramptastic turd-mobile?'

'I've told you before. Don't poke fun at poor people,' whispered Rosie's dad. Then he smiled at us. I don't think we were meant to have heard him. 'It's . . . really . . . er . . . *cute.*'

He said 'cute' like he really meant 'embarrassingly bad'.

Dad cleared his throat. 'We don't need anything flashy.'

Mr Taylor slapped Dad's arm yet again. 'Exactly! Only buy what you can afford. That's why I bought this beast. Cos I'm super-rich. Ha-ha-ha!'

Rosie, her dad and (to my horror) Vanya all cracked up laughing. Dad and I forced a smile.

'Only kidding!' guffawed Rosie's dad before stopping abruptly. 'Although just so you know, I *am* totally loaded.'

There was a long silence, then Rosie looked at her watch. 'We need to get moving like right now. I need to be at the first caravan site by lunchtime.'

'Ah yes,' said Dad, raising a finger. 'I noticed on the timetable that the caravan site is over a hundred miles *in the wrong direction*. And it's very expensive. Can't we find a cheaper one that's actually on the way to the wedding?'

'Absolutely not!' snapped Rosie. 'It's an important part of my journey, so that's where we're staying. *Hashtag*: end of. *Hashtag*: get over it. *Hashtag*: I'm the boss.'

*Typical Rosie*, I thought. *Nasty as always*.

But then a really weird thing happened. Mum

came out of Truckingham Palace with Mrs Taylor, who was telling her all about her shoe collection. As soon as Rosie saw my mum, she suddenly switched to being sweet and nice again.

'Oh, Mrs Garstang,' she simpered, 'it's totes amazetastic to be going on holiday with you.'

Mum smiled. 'Aww. Isn't she lovely, Roman?'

I was going to say: *she's about as lovely as a punch in the throat*. But I didn't have time, because right then there was a loud **KABOOM!** The ground shook and a huge ball of fire burst through the window of our caravan, sending shattered glass across the street.

'Gamble!' I cried.

'My caravan!' screamed Mum.

### Thirty Minutes Later – A Downgrade

We watched sadly as the fire engine trundled away down the street. They'd managed to put out the fire quite quickly but the caravan was wrecked. The kitchen was half-melted, most of the windows had been blown out by the explosion, and all the walls and carpets were ruined.

Gamble's face was black from the smoke and his

eyebrows and eyelashes had been burnt off. This made him look even weirder than normal, but although he'd been right next to the explosion, he wasn't hurt. The kid is completely indestructible. He's like one of those cockroaches that can survive a nuclear bomb.

'You know, I can't help but think it was a tiny bit my fault,' he sniffed, stroking Scratchy. The dog was also fine, although most of its hair had been singed off. It was all pink and stringy, like a piece of spaghetti with legs.

'A *tiny bit* your fault?' I said. 'It was *totally* your fault!'

Gamble looked hurt. 'I was trying to put the fireworks somewhere safe, innit.'

'Then why did you put them in the oven, Darren?' I asked.

'No one'd look in there.'

I considered this for a moment. 'Fair enough. But that doesn't explain why you turned the oven on full blast straight after.'

'Keep 'em warm,' he offered, wiping some of the soot off his face.

I put my head in my hands. The kid is beyond belief.

At that moment, Mum came out of the caravan, sobbing. '*Now* where will we stay?'

Mr Taylor followed her out. 'Could've been worse. He could've blown up Truckingham Palace.'

This didn't make us feel better.

Mum slowly turned to look at Rosie's dad. 'Talking of the motorhome, how many people can sleep in it?'

I realised here what she was suggesting. This was awful. I'd rather walk the four hundred miles to the wedding and sleep in the middle lane of the motorway than spend three nights cooped up with Rosie Taylor.

For once, Rosie saved the day.

'I'm soooooo sorrylicious, Mrs Garstang,' she said. 'It'd be super cool to stay with you but the spare room is like *jam-packed* with my clothes. Plus we don't have enough seatbelts, and we'd hate for Roman to get hurt if we had an accident.'

This wasn't true by the way. Rosie loves it when I get hurt. One time at school we had to write about our favourite memory. She wrote about when we went to the zoo in Year One and I got trampled on by a herd of camels.

'I understand,' said Mum, 'but we can't go to the wedding without somewhere to sleep.'

Rosie dragged me to one side. Once she was away from my mum, she was back to normal. 'I've tried to be nice and it hasn't worked. Tell your mad old mother to pull herself together. I am gonna have a FOFO if we don't get moving soon.'

'FOFO?' I asked.

'A full-on freak-out,' tutted Rosie, 'like when that American actress Lola Gunge shaved her head and attacked those Girl Guides with a tennis racquet.'

Why was she being so nice to my mum's face, then being horrible behind her back? It didn't make any sense. But this was Rosie. There had to be a reason.

'I'll make it up to you, Mrs Roman's mum,' said Gamble. 'Gizz your phone and I'll call Uncle Terry . . .'

## Uncle Terry

Ten minutes later, Mum, Dad, Gamble and I were standing with Gamble's Uncle Terry inside a new caravan.

Well, I say 'new'. It was actually about fifty years

old, and it smelled of a mixture of sour milk and rotten meat. The curtains were brown and tatty, the windows were green and cracked, and there was a sticker on the gas fire that said: 'DO NOT USE! DANGER OF DEATH!' It was also tiny – a poky lounge/kitchen, a toilet room the size of a shoebox and, well, nothing else.

'Whaddaya think?' asked Uncle Terry. I'd met Uncle Terry once before, when he kidnapped me while robbing our local shop. Since then he'd been in prison. According to Gamble, when Uncle Terry got out of jail last week, he'd decided to give up crime. He now had a business renting out his holiday caravan. We'd all thought that this was a stroke of luck . . . until we'd seen the caravan, that is.

'We'll take it!' announced Gamble.

Dad frowned. 'It's a bit cramped. And – *hang on* – is that a bloodstain on the carpet?'

Uncle Terry rubbed the red mark with his foot, which made the whole caravan bounce around. 'I'm pretty sure it's not *human* blood.'

'Rrrright,' said Dad, not convinced. 'What *is* it from, then?'

'Rat?' suggested Uncle Terry.

*Not* **really** *what we wanted to hear.*

'What about that hole in the roof?' asked Dad.

I looked up. There was a gap about the size of a person's head that you could see the sky through.

'Free air conditioning,' smiled Uncle Terry.

'What if it rains?' I asked.

He raised a finger. 'I'll throw in a free bucket and a couple of half-price rain jackets.'

Mum was in the kitchen area, peering inside the water tank. 'There's a dead hedgehog floating about in here.'

'See it as a big spiky ice cube,' grinned Uncle Terry.

Mum and Dad weren't impressed.

Uncle Terry held up his hands. 'Joke. I'll get rid of the hedgehog. And I'll look after Scratchy for our Darren so it can't mess the place up.'

I almost laughed. I mean, how could anything mess up this heap of crud?

Smiling kindly, Mum said, 'Thanks for showing it to us but I don't think so. What would the Taylors think?'

'Well,' said Uncle Terry, rubbing the back of his neck. He's a massive, scary-looking man, built like a polar bear. 'I've already unhooked it from my van and put your number plate on the back. So you've got to take it, really.'

Dad gulped. 'But . . .'

'You can't break off a deal,' said Uncle Terry, cracking his knuckles.

'Uncle Terry once set fire to someone who broke off a deal,' said Gamble unhelpfully.

'That's not true,' said Uncle Terry, wagging a finger at Gamble. 'I put him in a petrol-soaked sack and *threatened* to set fire to him. He changed his mind before I'd even struck a match. Big difference.'

Mum and Dad shuffled backwards.

Rosie's dad poked his head round the door. When he saw the inside of the caravan, his face screwed up in disgust. 'We need to get moving, people. Rosie needs time to get ready when we arrive.'

'Get ready for wh—' I began.

Rosie interrupted by knocking on the filthy front window. 'Please can we *like* go?'

Mum and Dad glanced at each other.

'Tell you what,' said Uncle Terry, sounding friendly again. 'You can borrow this caravan for free while I fix yours up. Wherever you are in the country, I'll bring it to you tomorrow morning and we'll swap. Promise.'

'Still no,' said Mum.

Dad squinted at him. '*Free*, you say?'

Dad loves a freebie.

'Do I look like a liar?' said Uncle Terry.

*Yes*, I thought, *you do*. But I wasn't about to say that to him, was I? I quite like being alive.

'Only for one night . . .' said Dad to Mum.

Mum huffed out her cheeks and walked out.

## A Seriously Long Journey

Within minutes, Uncle Terry had hooked the revolting old caravan up to our car and attached ours to his van. 'See you tomorrow,' he grinned, as Scratchy hopped into his passenger seat. I'm pretty certain he said the word 'suckers' under his breath as we pulled away.

Gamble and I were in the middle seats of the car. We'd tried to call his mum again to get rid of him but she didn't answer, and her voicemail message said: 'I'm not here. Leave me alone or I'll bite off your nose.'

We decided it was safer to take him with us.

Behind us, the back seats had been folded down and the boot was stuffed full of bags. Normally,

I'd be excited to go on holiday. But because of Vanya, Rosie, Gamble and the caravan, I felt completely miserable.

'You shouldn't have let him bully you,' hissed Mum, as Dad followed Truckingham Palace down our road. 'What will Rosie's parents think?'

Dad sighed. 'Did you see how scary he – **woah!**'

Gamble had suddenly leapt forward between the front seats to fiddle with the radio. Dad veered across the road. An oncoming car swerved out of the way, nearly mowing down a line of people at a bus stop.

Gamble didn't seem to notice. After a few twiddles, he found a station and turned it up to full volume. We were hit by a deafening blast of noise – booming drums, screeching guitars and ear-splitting screams. I felt like I was being punched in the brain. Gamble went crazy, leaping around the car and headbutting the windows.

'What *is* that?' cried Dad, turning the volume down most of the way.

Gamble twitched excitedly. 'Radio Brain Smash. Illegal radio station. Only plays the maddest thrash metal music, innit.'

Gamble is a massive fan of thrash metal music. If you've never heard of it before, it sounds a bit like a block of flats being demolished with all of the people trapped inside.

On the radio, the 'music' had stopped and a DJ was talking. He had a gruff voice like an iron bar being dragged through gravel. 'OK, you messed-up mutants,' he growled, 'that was "Sandpaper Your Grandma" by Babies With Rabies. They'll be playing at our secret festival, Smash Fest, which is gonna go off this weekend. Starting tomorrow, there'll be two days of non-stop loudness, with the scummiest bands, the freakiest people and the most violent headbanging.'

'Sounds amazing!' said Gamble.

It really didn't.

The DJ continued. 'Smash Fest is one hundred per cent against the law, so we ain't gonna tell you where it is yet. We don't want the cops or the fool who owns the land to come down and spoil the fun. So keep listening and we'll let you know the postcode one letter at a time. Now, crank up the noise cos here's The Exploding Eardrums with their mad new tune "Slaughter All Seagulls".'

'No thanks,' said Mum, flicking it off.

'Don't be tight!' howled Gamble. 'How are we gonna find out where the festival is?'

'We're not going to a music festival,' said Mum, 'we're going to a wedding. And by the way, Darren, I didn't see your bag. Did you bring your smart clothes?'

Gamble sniffed. 'Er . . . I'm wearing 'em.'

*Wow!* Gamble was dressed in a pair of filthy cut-off denim shorts and a black vest, which had a hazardous waste sign on it and the words, 'Touch me and die'.

'You mean,' said Mum slowly, 'you're going away for four nights and you've not brought a spare change of clothes?'

'Or underpants?' I asked.

'My pair's in the wash,' said Gamble, 'I was gonna borrow my brother Spud's but in the end I just thought, *Who needs 'em, right?*'

'Oh,' said Mum, sounding like she'd just swallowed some sick.

I shuddered, but I wasn't too surprised. When I first met him, Gamble proudly told me it was eight months since the last time he'd wiped his bottom.

Dad cleared his throat. 'How about a game? I spy with my little eye, something beginning with C.'

'Easy. Crushed cat,' called out Gamble, pointing at a poor animal in the gutter.

There was a long pause. 'I was actually thinking of "car",' said Dad. 'Maybe we *should* put your station back on after all.'

'Yesssss,' hissed Gamble, as the radio went back on at a low volume.

I closed my eyes and wrapped a jumper around my head to block out the throbbing background music and Gamble's ferocious dancing. But all I could think about was Vanya going off with Rosie and the awful caravan that was going to be our home for the night.

This was going to be a seriously long journey.

# Afternoon and Evening

## Gamble Takes on Rosie. And Wins

I must've fallen asleep because, the next thing I knew, Gamble was shoving a wet finger in my ear to wake me up.

'Yuck!' I cried.

'Calm down. It's just a bit of spit,' said Gamble.

I noticed a big letter P scribbled on the back of his hand. I was about to ask what it was when Mum said, 'Oooh. I knew the Taylors would take us somewhere special.'

We were following Truckingham Palace down a long driveway between perfectly trimmed hedges.

A sign read:

**LUSHTON MANOR LUXURY HOLIDAY PARK
AND COUNTRY CLUB
WHERE THE RIGHT TYPE OF PEOPLE
ARE ALWAYS WELCOME**

**WINNER OF ENGLAND'S LOVELIEST
HOLIDAY PARK AWARD 1991–PRESENT
UPCOMING EVENTS: *MODEL SEARCH*
REGIONAL FINAL**

'Looks expensive,' said Dad grumpily.

'Well,' said Mum, 'if we're going to be friends with the Taylors, we need to get used to splashing the cash.'

Dad and I said nothing.

We passed a snooty-looking man and woman who were trotting along the drive on equally snooty-looking horses. When they saw the caravan, they looked at us like we were dragging a dead skunk behind the car.

'Stop giving us evils!' snarled Gamble, pulling up his shirt and pressing his nipples against the window.

The horses reared up on their back legs, flailing

their front hoofs around. I sank down in my seat, covering my eyes.

Eventually, we reached a huge stone archway. Through it, we could see posh caravans and motorhomes just like Truckingham Palace dotted around rolling fields. There were tennis courts, a golf course and a lake with sailing boats bobbing up and down on it.

A man in a dark suit with gold buttons met Rosie's dad outside the motorhome. When he saw us, his face dropped.

'I'll hop out,' said Mum.

I wound down my window to listen in.

'Hello, er . . . *madam*,' said the man to Mum, 'are you wishing to stay or are you just turning around?'

He sounded like he hoped it wasn't the first one.

'Staying,' said Mum cheerfully.

The man winced like a chicken laying a really spiky egg. 'I'm . . . er . . . not sure we have space.'

Mum peered through the arch. 'That field's only got one caravan in it.'

'Ah. Well . . .'

'She's with me,' said Rosie's dad.

Raising one eyebrow, the man glanced from

Truckingham Palace to our rubbish caravan and back. Then he lowered his voice to Rosie's dad. 'Sir, we provide every service you could possibly need. There really was no need to bring your own servants.'

Rosie's dad laughed. 'She's not my servant. Although of course I *could* afford to pay her if I wanted to.'

The man laughed as if this was hilarious. 'Very good, sir. Now obviously you may have one of our premium pitches overlooking the lake. But we *do* have certain standards. I'm afraid your . . . er . . . *friends* must stay somewhere more . . . private.'

'Private?' asked Mum.

'Hidden from sight,' said the man.

Mum's mouth dropped open.

'Seems reasonable,' said Rosie's dad.

'Precisely, sir,' said the man, before turning to Mum. 'We have some very quiet spots, perfect for . . . er . . . *your sort*.'

'*Our* sort?' spluttered Mum.

'People on the – ahem – *budget* end of the market,' said the man, wringing his hands together.

'Poor people,' suggested Rosie's dad.

'Oh,' said Mum sourly.

'Come round to ours once you're parked,' said Mr Taylor, as Mum climbed back into our car. 'We'll cook lunch for you. Can't imagine your kitchen's very safe.'

Rosie leaned out of the driver's door of the motorhome. 'Hurry up, Dad! I've only got seven hours to get ready.'

'Coming, princess,' said Mr Taylor.

*Get ready for what?* I thought again, as Mum drove slowly round to our pitch.

## Lunch

The pitch they gave us was right next to the bins. It was horrible – the stink was almost as bad outside the caravan as it was inside. Plus, it was on such a steep slope that Dad had to put wooden blocks under the caravan's tyres to stop it rolling away.

I thought Mum was going to be annoyed about this, but she was way too excited that Rosie's parents had invited us over for lunch. She spent twenty minutes trying on different clothes before finally settling on the exact same outfit she'd been travelling in.

The rest of the campsite was really posh – full

of tanned families going for bike rides or playing badminton or carrying their golf clubs out towards the course. We stuck out like an angry zit but Mum didn't seem to notice.

'This is more like it,' she said excitedly, as we walked round to Truckingham Palace. 'Remember, we need to be well-behaved here. Especially if we want the Taylors to invite us on holiday again.'

I said nothing. If there was ever a reason *not* to be well-behaved, that was it. And anyway, Gamble doesn't understand 'well-behaved'. He ran on ahead, chasing squirrels and kicking parked cars.

Outside Truckingham Palace, there was a table loaded with bread rolls and salad (yuck). Meanwhile, Rosie's dad was cooking meat on a gas barbecue. It smelled *amazing*.

'How do you like your peacock burgers?' he said.

'*Peacock?*' I squeaked, losing my appetite. 'You mean one of those beautiful birds with the shiny blue feathers?'

Dad squinted. 'Isn't it a bit . . . *wrong* to eat them?'

'Nonsense!' said Rosie's dad. 'Tastes great. *Very* expensive.'

'My dad hit one in the car once,' grinned Gamble. 'It was delicious but the beak was well crunchy.'

'I'll just have the bun,' I said, feeling a bit ill.

'Where's Rosie?' asked Mum.

Her dad nodded towards the lake.

Rosie was standing on a little beach. She was wearing a pink dressing gown with 'PRINCE$$' written on it in gold letters, and her hair was in curlers. Vanya was filming her on an expensive-looking camera. I walked round to see what they were doing.

'Hi, fans,' cooed Rosie to the camera. 'Welcome to Rosie-dot-tv. As you can see, I'm getting ready for the . . . CUT! That little goat's winkle is ruining the shot.'

I realised she was talking about me.

Vanya lowered the camera and turned round to me. 'Hi, Roman.'

'I'm not *in* the shot,' I said, pretending I hadn't heard Vanya.

Rosie tutted. 'No, but I can see you, so obvs my face is going to look like I've just stepped in something revolting.'

'Sorry for being alive,' I said.

'You should be,' said Rosie. 'How am I supposed to get my fans excited if I've got to look at your horrible, lumpy head and . . . oh, *hi*, Mrs Garstang. So wonderlicious to see you!'

'Eh?' I said. It was like someone had flicked a switch to make Rosie nice again.

'Hello, Rosie,' smiled Mum. 'What are you up to?'

'Roman's just helping me make an ickle film for my new online TV channel.'

'Am I?'

'Awww. Isn't she a lovely girl, Roman? You two make a great team.'

'We sure do, Mrs G,' simpered Rosie.

I noticed Vanya shaking her head and rolling her eyes. Was she *jealous?*

'Well, I'll leave you to spend more time together,' Mum said, winking at me on the way past.

*Good grief.* What had got into her?

'Fancy some lunch, my little diamond?' said Rosie's dad, coming over.

Rosie looked at him like he'd just asked her to gargle a mouthful of fish guts. 'Absolutely not, you complete dimwit!' she snarled, back to her normal vile self. 'If I eat anything now I'll look like a massive whale in the competition.'

Rosie's dad didn't seem to notice how rude she was being. 'Good thinking, champ!'

'Competition?' I asked.

She ignored me. 'After I've done the video, I've got to put on my make-up. You'd better have bought me that new nail varnish I wanted, Dad. Because if you haven't I swear that when you're an old man I'll make you live in a rabbit hutch and I'll only feed you sawdust. Come on, Vanya. We'll film inside.'

She stormed off, with Vanya following her.

I walked back round to the side of the motorhome just as the door was slamming shut.

'I love how Rosie stands up for herself,' said Mum.

Rosie's mum smiled proudly. 'She's always like this before a beauty contest.'

'A *what*?!' I spluttered, unable to stop myself. Putting Rosie in a beauty contest would be like entering Gamble into the World's Cleanest Fingernails Competition. I don't want to be cruel, but she's got a head like a half-melted candle.

'Oh yes. Did we not mention? It's the regional finals for *Model Search* tonight,' said her mum. 'All the girls and boys get glammed up . . .'

'And they eliminate all the ugly ones so they can find the best-looking,' continued Rosie's dad, flipping a peacock burger with a hiss. 'The winner – AKA Rosie – will go on to the national final.'

*So* that's *why she'd made us drive all this way in the wrong direction.* Just so she could enter some stupid beauty contest.

It all made sense now.

I remembered seeing the competition advertised on the sign as we drove onto the site. It sounded awful to me – a whole roomful of vain people all posing and showing off – so it'd probably suit Rosie down to the ground.

'I'm sure she'll do well,' said Mum. 'She's very pretty, don't you think, Roman?'

I had no idea what to say to this. I've seen rotten onions that are prettier than her.

Rosie's dad put a plateful of burgers on the table. 'It's not the taking part; it's the winning that counts.'

I was pretty sure this was wrong.

The adults started filling their plates. Gamble snatched up a blood-soaked raw burger out of the packet and savaged it like a hungry shark. I sat off to the side on the grass, away from everyone else.

A few seconds later, Vanya slipped shyly out of the motorhome.

I didn't look at her.

She took a deep breath. 'I'm sorry for upsetting you.'

'Huh.'

'I need to expl—'

Rosie leaned out of the door. 'Vanya,' she hissed, quietly enough that the adults couldn't hear. 'You are *not* to talk to that awful little sweat-flannel. Come inside. *You've* got to get ready for the beauty contest too.'

Vanya froze. 'But I don't want to enter. I told you.'

'How else are you going to film me close up unless you're onstage? You're my guest so *hashtag*: do as you're told.' She clicked her fingers. 'Mother. Here. Now. Sort out Vanya.'

Before Vanya could argue, Rosie's mum was already leading her towards the motorhome to 'begin the transformation'.

'Hey! Can you do my make-up too?' said Gamble, trying to follow. 'I wanna look like a psycho-clown.'

Rosie looked horrified. 'Absolutely not. One, you're a boy. Two, these are expensive beauty products. One lipstick is probably worth more than your house. I'm not wasting them on making you look even more freakish. And three. Well, I don't want to be mean but . . .' she paused to look him up and down, 'you're the most disgust-amungous-looking swamp monster I've ever seen and you make me want to flip out my eyes with a spoon.'

*And that was her* not *wanting to be mean. Wow!*

Gamble looked like he was about to cry.

Meanwhile, Vanya was clinging to the doorframe of the motorhome while Rosie's mum peeled her fingers off one by one. 'Give it a try! You'll love looking like a princess!'

'I won't!' said Vanya. She's a tomboy who prefers football kits to dresses. I might even have felt sorry for her, if I wasn't so cross.

Mum called over to Mrs Taylor, 'Sorry. Did you say boys *and* girls could enter?'

'Oh yes!' replied Rosie's mum, as she finally shoved Vanya through the door. 'There's a winner for each.'

I didn't like how Mum looked off into space at this point.

'Panda sausages, anyone?' asked Mr Taylor, interrupting my thoughts. 'They're tasty *because* they're an endangered species.'

## Designer Outfit

We managed to avoid the panda sausages because Rosie had a humongous toddler tantrum when she couldn't find her hairspray. We could hear her snarling and spitting in the motorhome like a caged raccoon. Eventually, her dad had to drive to the nearest town in the sports car for an emergency replacement. We left them to it.

'Bit of an overreaction,' said Dad, as we walked away.

'Oh no,' said Mum, 'it's important for her to look her best.'

I said nothing. The only way Rosie could look her best would be to put a paper bag over her face.

None of us wanted to spend time in our caravan. Mum said she had things to do. I couldn't imagine what she might've been doing, but I didn't want to be with her anyway. Anyone who thinks Rosie Taylor is nice should be avoided at all costs.

Dad, Gamble and I went to the crazy golf course. I was absolutely useless; I could barely even hit the ball, let alone get it in the hole. And I wished I'd had a decent friend with me. Gamble was still in a grump about Rosie calling him ugly. It was totally not like him. At one point a rabbit stopped on the grass near us and he didn't even try to hit it with his golf club or anything.

When we got back to the caravan afterwards, Mum was waiting inside with a strange smile on her face. We ate cold tinned spaghetti out of the can because the cooker didn't work. Then Mum told Dad and me to get ready for the beauty contest.

'But I don't want to watch it,' I moaned.

'Me neither,' said Dad.

Mum tutted. 'We want to impress the Taylors, don't we?'

'Not particularly,' I said.

Mum pretended she hadn't heard. 'Where's Darren?'

'He was sad, so I let him listen to Radio Brain Smash in the car,' Dad said.

I was surprised Mum couldn't hear the music – the thudding drums were shaking the whole caravan.

'He'll give us a flat battery,' she said. 'Go and get him and I'll sort out your clothes.'

I found Gamble sitting in the car, holding a pen. This isn't usually a good thing. He has a serious graffiti habit; if you give him a pen he'll usually start writing rude words on everything. One time we got kicked off a bus after he drew a boob on the back of an old man's bald head.

I knocked on the window and he told me he'd be inside once he'd listened to the end of the tune. He looked a bit happier at least, but the song – 'Chronic Bumsplosion' by The Toilet Blockers – was giving me a headache, so I was glad to get away.

Unfortunately this feeling didn't last for long.

When I walked back into the caravan, I stopped in my tracks. Mum was proudly holding up the worst outfit I've ever seen – a pair of green-and-yellow checked trousers with a matching waistcoat, braces and bow tie.

'Ta-da!' she exclaimed.

'What the squashed chicken nugget is *that*?' I said. It was like something a talking mole would wear in a cartoon.

'It's your wedding outfit,' she grinned. 'I bought it the other day. Thought I'd surprise you!'

*Surprise me?* She almost gave me a heart attack.

I felt myself sweating. I'd thought I'd be wearing normal stuff to the wedding. 'Tell me you're kidding. I can't wear *that*! It'll blind people.'

'But it's from an expensive shop.'

'Clothes shop or joke shop?' I asked, completely serious.

Mum pursed her lips. 'Look. If we're going to be friends with the Taylors, we need to wear designer clothes.'

'Just because clothes are expensive, it doesn't mean they're good,' I said. This is true by the way – Rosie Taylor's clothes cost loads of money and half the time she looks like she's been dressed by an alien.

'It was on special offer,' said Mum. 'Ninety-nine per cent off.'

'Only because nobody else in the world would ever wear it. And hang on,' I said, a horrible feeling building up in my guts, '*why* have you got it out now?'

'You need to dress smartly to watch Rosie in her contest.'

'You want me to go out in public like that?!' I cried. 'People will think I've gone mad.'

'Don't be silly. This is important. We need the Taylors to know that we enjoy doing the same things as them. That way they'll want to be our friends. And you should be supporting Rosie – you and her look lovely together.'

'We do not!' I cried. I did not like the sound of *that* one bit. 'I'm not going tonight. And I'm not wearing *that*!'

'I thought you might say that,' said Mum. 'So I bought these at the campsite shop . . .'

Then, as cool as you like, she reached into the cupboard, pulled out a cardboard box and flipped open the lid.

'Dough-ly moley,' I whispered.

The tray contained twelve plump, sticky Squidgy Splodge raspberry jam doughnuts. My favourites!

Oh my word, they looked gorgeous – the sugar on top glistening like crushed diamonds. The ruby-red jam trickling out of the sides. The holes in the sides like little mouths whispering to me: *Eat us, Roman. Eat usssss . . .*

Licking my lips, I reached forward to grab one, but she pulled the box out of my grasp. 'Ah – ah – ah,' she said. 'Only if you come and watch the competition. In your wedding outfit.'

'What if I don't want to?'

'Then they're going straight in the bin.'

Surely this was bribery. Cruelty. Torture. How could anyone threaten to destroy something so beautiful? There must be laws against it. What would she threaten to do next – strangle a dolphin? Drop a nuclear bomb on a kitten?

I couldn't bear to see this happen.

With a low growl, I snatched the clothes off her.

At that moment Gamble came back inside the caravan. The pen was tucked behind his ear and he was bouncing about excitedly. 'Cool clothes,' he said. 'The drummer from Zombie Grandad and The Brain-Sucking Freaks wears stuff like that. He keeps live moles in the pockets of the waistcoat then eats 'em onstage.'

That didn't make me feel any better.

'I'm glad *someone* appreciates fine clothes,' said Mum.

'What's that on your hand, Darren?' I said. There was some fresh writing on there and I was desperate to change the subject.

He covered it quickly. 'This? Nothing. *Doughnuts!* Wow! I'll have one or ten.'

'You won't,' I said. I'd rather have let him eat my feet than eat my doughnuts. And if I had to earn them by wearing these dreadful togs then no one else was getting a single crumb.

'There'll be plenty to go round,' said Mum. '*After* we've watched the competition.'

The thought of seeing Rosie onstage made me feel ill. But what choice did I have? If I didn't go, Mum would bin the doughnuts. Plus I'd have to sit in the caravan all evening and wait to see what happened first: would I catch a disease off the cushions or would the whole thing fall to pieces and crush me?

Sadly, what actually happened was much worse than either of these possibilities.

## Beauty Contest

'I look like an idiot,' I said, outside the clubhouse. After making me get clean in the shower block, Mum had spent ages combing the tangles out of my curly hair. Then I'd been forced to put on the outfit of doom.

'You look *handsome*,' she replied. 'Just do as you're told and the doughnuts are yours.'

My stomach gurgled. I hadn't had one since my pre-breakfast snack that morning.

Inside the clubhouse was seriously swanky – all wood-panelled walls and thick plum-coloured carpet. There were about two hundred people in there. Waiters in bow ties buzzed around the tables, balancing trays of drinks on one hand. At the far end, a single spotlight was pointing at a sort of stage/dance-floor area. There was a microphone and a big banner that read:

# *MODEL SEARCH*
## BEAUTY CONTEST

## IT'S WHAT'S ON THE
## OUTSIDE THAT COUNTS

I wanted to sit in a dark corner, but Rosie's parents waved at us from a table by the front and Mum dragged us over.

'The girls are backstage getting ready,' smiled Rosie's dad. 'You're lucky you didn't miss any of it.'

'Really lucky,' said Dad flatly. Mum shot him an angry look.

'They both look gorgeous!' gushed Rosie's mum. 'Well. Obviously Rosie looks a lot *more* gorgeous but . . . you know . . . good girl, Vanya, for trying.'

I imagined Vanya had probably tried everything *not* to be a part of it.

'Why did Rosie enter the contest?' asked Gamble.

I could see his point. I'm not trying to be cruel but the other girls would have to look like deformed donkeys for Rosie to have a chance of winning.

Rosie's mum pursed her lips. 'To prove she's the most beautiful girl on the planet, of course.'

*Perhaps she is*, I thought, *Just not* **this** *planet. Maybe there's another planet out in space where everyone else looks like massive puddles of bubbling sludge* . . .

Gamble sniffed and stared off into the distance. 'To prove she's beautiful, eh? Can I go back to the caravan?'

'Not on your own, no,' said Mum.

'Awww. I'll only be ten minutes.'

'Let him go,' said Rosie's mum. Then, in a lower voice: 'He's making the place look cheap.'

Mum sighed. 'All right. Be quick. I'll get the keys from my bag.'

'No need,' said Gamble, holding them up. 'I've already pinched 'em.'

Before Mum could say anything, he'd run off.

Immediately, some terrible song about being beautiful started blaring out over the sound system and the multicoloured stage lights began flashing.

An oldish woman in a glittery dress tottered onto the stage. 'Good evening,' she cooed. At a guess, I'd say she had about three million teeth, each of them massive and brilliant white. 'And welcome to the *Model Search* regional finals.'

There was loud applause from the crowd. Rosie's dad yelled, 'Smash 'em to bits, Rosie!' Even though we hadn't seen her yet.

'I'm your host, Andrea Rhodes, and here are our judges . . .'

Everyone clapped again as three elderly people – two women and a man – sat down at the table by the side of the stage.

'I tried to give the judges some money to make sure Rosie won, but apparently that's against the rules,' whispered Rosie's dad, clearly disappointed.

Andrea Rhodes continued: 'Soon we'll meet the contestants all at the same time. Then they'll chat to you one by one. After that, two of them will be crowned the champions. They'll go on to the national finals, which could be the springboard to fame and fortune. Our previous winners have included the actress Melanie Chuff, the pop star Gary Gunk, and the supermodel Fiona Bunkbed.'

'*Ooooh*,' said the audience.

Rosie's mum clapped her hands together. 'Fame and fortune, here we come!'

*I wouldn't hold your breath*, I thought.

'Please welcome your contestants,' said Andrea Rhodes.

There was a loud cheer as three girls walked onto the stage. They were all wearing horrible ruffly, sparkly dresses, with tiaras balanced on their heads. Their enormous smiles were framed with bright red lipstick.

A moment or two later, Vanya trudged after them in a huge orange dress that made her look like a giant satsuma. She'd kept her AstroTurf boots on underneath though, and she was still carrying the camera. If I hadn't still been cross, I might've felt sorry for her – she obviously didn't want to be there.

'Rosie gave Vanya the worst dress she owns,' said Mrs Taylor proudly.

'Win at all costs,' smiled Rosie's dad. 'It's the Taylor family motto.'

'Of course,' Dad said.

The girls lined up at the front to curtsey to the crowd. I was wondering where Rosie was when she dramatically burst out from backstage.

She was wearing a long, floaty blue cape like a superhero or (more like it) a witch. Striding across the front, she held her arms out so that the other girls were hidden behind it. After standing on three of the girls' feet, she grabbed the presenter's microphone.

'Hi, fans!' she cooed. 'I'm Rosie Taylor. But you probably already knew that. Thanks for coming all this way just to see me. And . . . OI! VANYA! You're meant to be filming me!'

Looking thoroughly cheesed off, Vanya did as she was told.

'I've brought my personal camerawoman to film my journey,' explained Rosie, pouting for the camera. 'I got her to enter the contest so she could get really close to the action. Big shout out to all my online fans too. I'm gonna bring the trophy home just for you! Mwah mwah!'

The presenter politely yanked the microphone off her and tried to smile. 'So we have our girls. But our only boy hasn't arrived yet. Is he here?'

At first this comment didn't mean anything to me.

But then Mum was standing up.

Then she was waving towards the front.

Then she was pulling me to my feet.

And then she was calling: 'Coo-ee! Here he is!'

My blood ran cold.

Then I realised. *That's* where she'd disappeared to earlier. She'd been entering me into this beauty contest. How could I have been so stupid?

'I'm not doing it!' I wailed, fighting to sit down.

Mum wrestled me back to my feet. 'But you're lovely and handsome. Imagine how great it'd be if you and Rosie won together!'

'Why didn't you tell me?'

'I'd never have got you through the door,' said Mum, before waving towards the presenter. 'He's coming!'

The spotlight spun round, dazzling my eyes.

'Don't be shy. Give him a round of applause!' said the presenter.

I was trying to squirm against Mum, but she and the presenter were hauling me onto the stage by my waistcoat. Everyone in the room was clapping. Apart from Rosie, of course. She was staring poison daggers at me.

'Think about the doughnuts,' Mum whispered, before rushing back to her seat. The presenter squeezed my hand tightly so that I couldn't escape.

This was awful.

But if there's one thing I've learned, it's that things can always get worse.

'Well,' said the presenter, not letting go of me. 'We've got our one handsome boy and our five gorgeous girls.'

'SIX!' came a scream from the back of the room.

I couldn't exactly see who'd shouted out because of the glaring stage lights, but I'd recognise that voice anywhere.

'Ex-*cuse* me?' said the presenter, peering into the audience. For the first time, her smile faded as the sixth girl marched onto the stage.

## The Sixth Girl

'But you can't just . . . *enter*!' spluttered Andrea Rhodes. Half the audience were sniggering. The other half were muttering angrily. The judges looked like they were about to keel over.

And all because the sixth girl was none other than Darren Gamble.

Seriously. Gamble. The world's grossest boy had entered himself into a beauty contest. As a girl. It was completely crazy: like entering a tomato into the world's tastiest food competition.

He was wearing my mum's flowery skirt, pulled right up over his belly, and his clumpy boots. Pink lipstick was smeared across his face. Worst of all, though . . .

'Hang on!' exclaimed Mum from the audience. 'Is that my *bra*?!'

*Yuck!* How could he even *touch* such a disgusting thing, let alone *wear* it?

'Is this thing on?' he said into the microphone, before yelling, 'SWEATY KNICKERS!' at the top of his voice.

Andrea Rhodes snatched it away from him. 'You can't enter the girls' competition. You're a boy.'

'Can't prove it!' Gamble said calmly. 'My name's Susan. Someone said I was proper ugly and I want to prove how beautiful I am.'

'Why don't you just enter the boys' competition, then?' asked Andrea Rhodes.

Gamble scratched his neck. 'I quite like wearing a skirt. I can feel the breeze around my knees. And this bra's well comfy.'

The kid's a nutter.

The presenter scurried over to the judges' table and they had a muttered conversation. The occasional muffled phrase got picked up by the microphone.

'If *that's* a girl, I'm a bicycle . . .'

'*You* get rid of it then. I'm not touching it . . .'

'Probably bite us if we get too close . . .'

'Not like he's going to win, though . . .'

'Yes. Weird-looking thing, isn't he . . .'

'Head like a half-chewed peanut balanced on a cocktail stick . . .'

'Fine. Let's get this over with.'

Andrea Rhodes turned, smiling, back to the audience as though nothing had just happened. 'Ladies and gentlemen,' she announced, 'I give you our one boy and our . . . ahem . . . *six* girls.'

I stood there, completely humiliated, while Gamble and the girls smiled and fluffed their hair. Vanya shuffled behind everyone so she couldn't be seen. Rosie elbowed a few girls out of the way and pushed to the front. And Gamble picked his nose and wiped it on the presenter's dress.

We were made to stand at the back of the stage. Then we were called up one at a time to be asked questions.

The girls were all nice, although they seemed to be made entirely out of lipstick, glitter and hairspray. They were also all able to speak without moving their lips – the whole time they were onstage they kept their mouths fixed in these incredible grins that you could drive a train through. And they weren't exactly what you'd call clever.

Here are some of the answers they gave (I don't think I need to tell you the questions):

'I want to be a celebrity. But if I can't be a celebrity . . . ooh . . . I'd probably just be a *different type* of celebrity.'

'Does wearing nice clothes count as a hobby?'

'Oh. Erm. I think I like maths? That's the one with the numbers and those funny squiggly lines, isn't it? One add one is four and all that stuff.'

After that, it was Vanya's turn. When she was asked what she'd like to be when she grew up, Vanya replied, 'A footballer. Or maybe a builder.'

Andrea Rhodes looked at Vanya as if she'd just said she'd like to kick puppies for a living.

After Vanya, Gamble clomped to the front. Some of the audience laughed and whistled at him but most people seemed a little angry that he was there.

'So . . . *Susan*,' said Andrea Rhodes, 'what do you want to be when you grow up?'

'Half-man, half-robot,' said Gamble confidently. 'With metal hooks for hands, X-ray eyes and laser guns instead of nipples.'

He demonstrated this last bit by making guns with his fingers, then sticking them into Mum's bra and making *pyeeeuuu-pyeeeuuu* noises.

'Right,' said Andrea Rhodes.

Gamble wasn't finished yet though. 'Either that or I'd like to get bitten by a radioactive rat.'

'What?'

'Cos then I'd turn into a giant rat-boy the size of a house and I could live in a sewer and bite everyone I didn't like, or my fleas could give 'em all diseases.'

The presenter looked exasperated. 'Ladies and gentlemen – *ahem* – Susan.'

Gamble sauntered off, wiggling his bottom. A couple of people cheered.

The final competitor was Rosie Taylor. Vanya started filming as Rosie strutted to the front of the stage like she owned the place.

'Before we start, can I just say *what was that?*' said Rosie. 'I mean, I thought the other girls were bad but *that* little freak was worse than the rest of them put together.'

'Spot on! Let 'em know who's boss!' bellowed her dad.

The rest of the audience weren't quite so pleased

though. At the back of the stage, the lights were less dazzling, so I could see out into the audience. Some people were whispering to each other. Most looked a bit shocked. The people who I guessed were the parents of the other girls were the angriest. They *really* didn't like hearing Rosie insult their children.

'So,' said the presenter, 'why should you win?'

'Well, I'm not being horrible,' said Rosie, which is always a sign that she's about to be extremely horrible. 'But girl number one looked like a cheesy Wotsit in a dress. Number two had a backside the size of France. And as for number three . . . *Yikes!* Her pet rabbit called and it wants its teeth back. *Hashtag*: goof alert!'

Apart from Rosie's parents – who whooped and yelled: 'That's my girl!' and 'You tell 'em!' – the whole room seemed utterly stunned, and the atmosphere was becoming quite menacing.

'Boot her out!' cried one person.

'Turn off the microphone!' shouted someone else.

'O to the M to the G! Listen to the haters,' said Rosie, holding up her palm to the audience. 'Maybe if you lot were a bit nicer, your daughters wouldn't have turned out so grim-looking. Nasty people have ugly kids. Fact.'

The crowd began to boo, and the presenter bundled Rosie to the back of the stage.

After her, it was my turn. The presenter pulled me to the front and said: 'That's an interesting outfit. If I wanted to buy clothes like that – for instance, if I needed to dress a large teddy bear – where would I get them?'

I totally froze, unable to speak. My cheeks were burning and my mouth wouldn't work. It was awful. After seven more questions from her and embarrassing silence from me, Andrea Rhodes gave up and moved on to the results. As I walked to the back of the stage, Vanya gave me a little smile. I ignored her and scuttled into the shadows.

### And the Winner is . . .

Obviously, I won the boys' competition. This is nothing to be proud of. Even Andrea Rhodes said, 'Well, there was no one else we could give it to,' as she plonked a crown on my head and draped a sash over my shoulder.

I looked at my shoes.

Mum thought that this was the greatest thing that had ever happened though. She started sobbing: 'I always knew you were the most handsome boy on earth!'

Rosie glared at me like she wanted to pull off all my limbs.

After that, I hid at the side of the stage again. They got the girls and Gamble to stand at the front. All of them were applauded loudly by the audience. Well, apart from Vanya, Gamble and Rosie, that is. Vanya was given a quiet clap, Gamble got a mixture of cheers and grumbles, and Rosie was solidly booed.

'Make sure you're filming my big moment,' Rosie ordered Vanya, 'I'm going to get so many new subscribers it's untrue.'

Vanya wearily did as she was told.

A judge handed Andrea Rhodes a gold, sparkly envelope. The other judges stood alongside, holding a huge bunch of flowers and a pink sash with 'WINNER!' written on it.

'What a contest,' gushed the presenter. 'So difficult to choose a champion.'

'Yeah right,' snorted Rosie's dad.

'But we must. So . . .'

Andrea Rhodes opened the envelope. Apart from Vanya (who seemed completely bored) and Rosie (who was pouting confidently) the girls looked nervous. Most nervous of all was Gamble. Crossing his fingers, his face was screwed up like a pug sucking on a lemon.

'The winner is . . .'

Before Andrea Rhodes had chance to announce the name, Rosie burst forward, pulled the sash over her head and grabbed the microphone and flowers. Weeping, she said, 'Thank you, fans. I can't tell you how much this means to Rosie Taylor. When Rosie Taylor is famous, Rosie Taylor will remem—'

The presenter wrestled the microphone off her. 'Stop it!' she hissed. 'You didn't win!'

Rosie staggered backwards like she'd just been headbutted in the lungs. 'WHAT?!'

She swiped the envelope off the presenter and tore it open. 'You mean . . . *that* dumpy little goblin won?!' she cried, pointing at the cheesy Wotsit in a dress, who didn't know whether to look delighted or insulted. 'Hashtag: joke.'

I glanced at Vanya, who was trying not to smile.

'STOP FILMING ME!' Rosie screamed at her.

The judges were attempting to remove the sash from round her neck, but Rosie ducked away from them.

'Hang on!' she cried, turning back to the results. 'You put Rosie Taylor in *last* place. Have you got no eyes? You think I'm less beautiful than *that*!'

She pointed an accusing finger at Gamble, who grinned like an excited chimp as he jiggled Mum's bra up and down with his hands. 'Check me out! I'm the fifth hottest babe on the planet!'

'NNNNNNNNNNNNOOOOOOOOOOOOOOOO OOOOO!' screamed Rosie. Then, still wearing the winner's sash, she jinked out from under the judge's grasp and made a run for it, yelling: 'MAKE WAY FOR THE PEOPLE'S CHAMPION!'

Unfortunately for her though, the actual winner of the contest wasn't going to let her escape quite so easily. As Rosie zigzagged through the crowd, the cheesy Wotsit rugby-tackled her, smashing her into a table in an explosion of glasses and drinks.

The crowd fell silent.

'Vicious!' said Gamble. 'I love it!'

## An Incident

There followed what can only be described as 'an incident'.

> After she'd been rugby-tackled, there was a massive fight involving Rosie, her mum, the cheesy Wotsit's whole family, Andrea Rhodes and all three of the elderly judges.

$$\downarrow$$

> In the end, Vanya used her karate skills to pin Rosie down and save everybody else. I have to admit this was pretty cool. Afterwards, one of the judges had to go to hospital to have a sunflower stalk removed from his left nostril. Then . . .

$$\downarrow$$

> Rosie's dad tried to make them do the whole contest again, claiming that the result shouldn't stand because Gamble had entered. This led to more pushing and shoving, which only ended when Rosie's mum threatened to sue someone 'so hard that in

a hundred years her great-grandchildren
would still be living in a cardboard box and
eating dog food.'

↓

While everyone was fighting, Gamble
sneaked round the tables drinking
wine and beer out of their glasses.
Seriously – *wine and beer*. He's only
ten. Within a couple of minutes –
completely drunk – he'd picked up
the microphone and was hanging
one-handed off the glitter-ball above
the stage, singing a rude song about
a naked donkey.

↓

As we watched this, open-mouthed, Andrea
Rhodes pulled the sash off my shoulders
and snarled: 'And you're disqualified!'
Although this made no sense, I couldn't
have cared less. Mum was begging her to
change her mind when . . .

↓

The lights in the room came on. The man who'd met us earlier at the entrance stormed over and told us we had ten minutes to be off the site or he'd call the police. 'There's no need to kick us out,' said Mum. But then there was a loud ripping sound as Gamble wrenched the mirrorball out of the ceiling. It hit the ground and shattered into a million pieces with Gamble lying on top of it, laughing like a maniac. 'We'll be on our way then,' said Dad.

Shortly afterwards, we sheepishly followed Truckingham Palace off the campsite. A large crowd gathered to shake their fists at us as we left. Someone even threw an egg. Gamble, who was still wearing Mum's bra, mooned drunkenly out of the window at them and cackled as we disappeared into the night.

# SATURDAY

# Morning

## We Go Shopping and Gamble Takes Control

'Wake up!' yelled Gamble, before sitting on my head and trumping violently.

I shoved him off and opened one gluey eye. 'What time is it?'

'Half five,' he said cheerfully.

Half past five? In the morning? On a Saturday? What would he do next – pull out my teeth with a set of pliers? I rolled over. 'Wake me up in six hours.'

Something disgusting and wet touched my face. I leapt up in the air, flicking it off. 'What was that?'

'My new best mate, Slimy Trevor,' he said, rooting round on the floor, then holding up the biggest, fattest slug I've ever seen. 'There was a nest of 'em in my shoes.'

Slugs! Yuck! This caravan was absolutely vile. As well as the slugs, water was literally pouring down the walls from the hole in the ceiling. It'd started chucking it down as soon as we'd left the campsite and hadn't stopped since. The end of my sleeping bag was so soggy my feet had gone wrinkly.

I narrowed my eyes. 'A *nest* of slugs? Where are the rest of them?'

'You don't wanna know,' sniffed Gamble. Something about the way he picked his teeth and licked his lips made me think he was probably right – I *really* didn't want to know.

Mum and Dad were still asleep on the floor by the little kitchen. Gamble and I had slept on the fitted sofa, which hadn't been folded out because there wasn't space. It was so narrow I'd fallen out of bed about eight times, and it was about as comfortable as lying on a sack of coconuts.

A car whooshed past outside, shaking the whole caravan. After leaving Lushton Manor, we'd driven on in the torrential rain and stopped at the first place we could find – a lay-by at the side of a busy road.

'Why are you up at this crazy time anyway?' I yawned.

'Uncle Terry phoned my mobile. He'll be here in a minute with your caravan.'

At last – some good news. Things were finally looking up.

Right then, a horn beeped and a van pulled up behind us.

## The Return of Uncle Terry

Dad blearily staggered to the door in his pyjamas.

'Morning, squire!' said Uncle Terry, squeezing past him and practically filling the room. 'There's something on your face.'

Dad reached up and pulled a slug off his cheek. Squirming, he tossed it into the sink.

Gamble fished it out and put it in his pocket. 'All right, Uncle Terry. How's Scratchy?'

'He's fine,' said Uncle Terry, 'I left him at home with a big bag of crisps, a bowl full of Coke and a pack of his favourite cigarettes to eat.'

'Wow,' I said.

'How did you all sleep?'

Mum had one eye completely closed, and the other was only open a crack. 'I think a mouse may have been in my sleeping bag.'

'Well, your caravan's out back, clean and ready,' he smiled, handing Mum a piece of paper. 'Just the small matter of your bill.'

Mum looked confused. 'Bill? But you said it was free.'

'Oh no. Borrowing *this* caravan was free,' said Uncle Terry. 'But there's a teeny-tiny fee for cleaning *your* caravan and bringing it back.'

'What do you mean by *teeny-tiny*?' asked Mum, squinting.

'Eight thousand pounds!' squeaked Dad, reading over her shoulder. 'That's more than our new caravan cost in the first place!'

Uncle Terry sniffed. 'Man's got to eat.'

'What do you eat?' said Dad. 'Diamonds on toast?'

Uncle Terry's eyes narrowed dangerously. 'I don't like the way you're talking to me.'

'Uncle Terry once ripped off a man's arms because he didn't like the way he talked to him,' said Gamble.

'You make me sound like an animal, Darren,' said Uncle Terry. 'That was only *one* arm I pulled off. And they sewed it back on. It works almost as well as it did before.'

Mum glanced at Dad. 'But we don't *have* that much money.'

Uncle Terry sucked his teeth. 'No problem. You don't have to pay a penny.'

'Phew!' said Dad, 'That's really ki—'

'But I'll keep *your* caravan.'

'What?'

'Seems fair to me,' shrugged Gamble.

'Don't worry,' said Uncle Terry, 'you can have this one for nothing. I'll sell yours to pay off what you owe me.'

'But . . . you can't . . .' spluttered Dad.

Uncle Terry sighed patiently. 'You just said that your caravan is worth *less* than the eight thousand pounds you owe me.'

'But I don't think we *do* owe you eight thousand pounds,' said Mum.

'Not what it says on the bill,' said Uncle Terry, holding out his hands. 'Call it a present for looking after our Darren so well. Have a lovely holiday.'

And before anyone could stop him, he was out of the door, back in his van and off down the road with our caravan behind.

So that was that. We were stuck in this pile of trash. But things got even worse when we went to get our breakfast. The mouse that had kept Mum awake was now inside the doughnut box, along with half its family. Mice! Eating my doughnuts. Even I wasn't going to touch them now. Mum screamed. Dad shut the box quickly and threw it in the bin in the lay-by.

'Aw!' whined Gamble. 'I'd have eaten 'em.'

I wasn't sure if he was talking about the doughnuts or the mice.

Dad patted his heart. 'We'll have to go next door and see if the Taylors can spare any food.'

'But they already think we're complete tramps,' said Mum.

'No way am I begging off Rosie,' I said.

'I'm sure Rosie's mum mentioned that she'd bought doughnuts from the shop too,' said Dad.

*MORE DOUGHNUTS?!*

'I'll get dressed,' I said quickly.

Five minutes later, we all trooped over to Truckingham Palace, which was parked in front of us. Dad knocked on the door. The smell of bacon and eggs seeped out through an open window, making my stomach ache.

'You'll have to let yourselves in!' called Rosie's dad.

Dad pushed a button by the side of the *Star Wars* door. There was a hissing noise, the door slid open and we stepped inside. And **sweet Squidgy Splodge!** It was incredible.

## Inside Truckingham Palace

If our caravan was like Gamble's dog, Scratchy – smelly, disgusting and likely to give you a disease, then Truckingham Palace was more like a royal cat – elegant and sleek with a massive TV in the middle.

OK, so maybe not the TV, but you get what I mean.

I spun round on the spot to take it all in: sparkling tiled floor; driver's dashboard with more buttons and screens than a spaceship; reclining leather seats for the driver and passenger which spun round to face into the huge lounge; L-shaped leather sofa opposite a TV about the size of our whole caravan; shiny metal kitchen with an enormous fridge.

'Great to see you!' said Rosie's dad as though it really wasn't. He strode down the caravan in his bathrobe, smoking a disgusting cigar. 'Shame you're late for breakfast. I ate all the bacon and Rosie threw the doughnuts away cos they're too fattening.'

My stomach actually cried when he said this.

He noticed Mum and Dad looking round at the motorhome.

'You get what you pay for, right?' Rosie's dad said smugly, 'Everything you see is voice-activated or controlled from this tablet. TV . . .'

He picked up the tablet, jabbed the screen and the TV flicked on.

'*Ooooh*,' we all said.

'Disco . . .'

With a swipe of his finger, the blinds came slowly down, plunging the room into darkness. Then he tapped the tablet again. Some funky music blared out of hidden speakers and lights flashed around the room.

'*Ooooh*,' we all said again.

He swiped the screen once more and the room returned to normal. 'We can even make it bigger . . .'

With one more tap of the screen, sections of the wall on both sides of the motorhome just slid outwards. Honestly. It was unreal – the room grew about six feet wider, just like that.

'*Ooo-ooo-ooooh*,' we all said.

'Awesome!' said Gamble, grabbing at his sleeve. 'Can I have a go?'

'Absolutely not,' said Rosie's dad, holding the tablet up out of his reach before turning to my dad.

'These are just a few of the features. The tablet has voice-activated SatNav that can take you anywhere in the world. Bit smarter than what you're used to, eh?'

'We prefer things small and cosy,' said Dad.

'Course you do,' smiled Rosie's dad, slapping him on the arm for the millionth time. Dad seemed to be getting a bit fed up with this.

'Can you get Radio Brain Smash?' said Gamble, clinging to Mr Taylor's wrist like an aggressive wart.

Rosie's dad tried to shake him off. 'Radio *what*?'

'It's like having a bomb going off inside your skull,' I said.

Gamble grinned like this was actually a good thing. 'It's coming live from a secret music festival. Can I listen or what? Please please please.'

'If I said *yes,* would you promise to never touch me again?' said Rosie's dad, looking at Gamble as though he was made entirely out of rat vomit.

'Brownie's honour,' said Gamble, saluting.

Rosie's dad gave him a set of wireless headphones and stroked the tablet again. 'Right. Don't break anything.'

Gamble put them on. 'Oh YESSSS! The Dirty Nappies are playing!'

We left him headbanging round the room as Rosie's dad led us along the motorhome, showing off about all of the different rooms. When he opened the last door, he said 'Whoops!'

In the bathroom, Rosie was sitting in a round, bubbling Jacuzzi, drinking orange juice from a wine glass. Luckily she was wearing a swimming costume and the bubbles covered everything I wouldn't want to see. Vanya was filming her from the side.

'CUT!' screamed Rosie, and Vanya switched off the camera. 'Daddy, you brainless bogbrush! Why are you letting *this* freak in here?'

'What have I done this time?' I sighed.

She tutted. 'First you invited that little gross-osaurus Darren Gamble on *my* special trip. Then you must've brainwashed the judges of the beauty contest. I've never been so humiliated in all my life.'

'Isn't it sweet? They're having a little lovers' tiff,' said Mum, coming in.

'A *what*?!' I said.

'You're so cute together!' she giggled.

What was she talking about? Had the woman finally gone mad?

Rosie's mouth opened wide in horror. And then something weird happened. She stopped, and a strange smile grew on her lips. 'Of course . . .' she said, 'Cute.'

But before I could ask her what on earth she meant, she'd ducked herself under the water.

'All right, Roman?' said Vanya, embarrassed.

I nodded but didn't smile. I wanted her to know I was still cross.

Rosie's dad led us out of the bathroom, where we bumped into Mrs Taylor. 'Look at your hair!' she said to my mum. 'You look like a homeless sheep.'

'Thanks,' said Mum.

'Don't worry. We'll find an emergency hairdresser in town who can turn you into a movie star.'

Mum shivered with excitement. 'Oooh! Really?'

'Hmm,' said Dad, 'about the plans for today . . .'

'Do you need a hand reading them?' asked Rosie's mum, seriously.

'No,' said Dad. 'It says we're going to drive four hundred miles with a break in the middle to go shopping. For five hours.'

*Five hours of shopping with Rosie?* Good grief. I'd rather spend the day giving myself paper cuts on the eyeballs.

'Won't it be wonderful!' simpered Rosie's mum, clapping her hands together.

Rosie emerged from the Jacuzzi like a radioactive sea monster. She wrapped herself in a robe and came out into the corridor, followed by Vanya. 'You'd better have your credit card, Daddy,' Rosie said, 'I need to spend spend spend!'

'Anything for my princess,' said her dad.

'There might be a park in the town,' said Vanya hopefully. 'Roman and I could play football while you shop.'

Even though I'm about as good at football as a mouldy lump of cheese, this sounded all right to me. Well, apart from spending time with Vanya, that is. I wasn't going to forgive her that easily.

'Www.nochance.com,' said Rosie. 'Rosie Taylor does not *do* sports. Imagine if something tragic happened, like I broke a nail. The internet would literally explode. Anyway. You've got to film me shopping. I'm up to two hundred thousand subscribers.'

Vanya huffed out her cheeks.

Dad frowned. 'But we spent all our money on our new caravan.'

'That's OK,' smiled Rosie's mum kindly, 'You can watch us spend our money instead. It'll be fun.'

This really didn't sound like fun to me.

'I thought you already had loads of clothes in the bedrooms,' I said to Rosie.

Rosie tutted. 'Literally everyone on earth is talking about what Rosie Taylor is going to be wearing to this wedding.'

'I'm not sure they are . . .' I said.

'Hashtag: Rosie'snewweddingoutfit is trending worldwide. If I don't rock up in something amazing, my reputation will be in tatters.'

'You should be more supportive of Rosie,' said Mum to me.

I rolled my eyes.

'Now,' Rosie continued, 'everyone into the lounge. I've scheduled another video call with Lee and Kat.'

## Job

Mum, Dad and I were first into the lounge. We found Gamble scribbling something on his hand again. I tried to ask him about it but he turned up the volume on the headphones and bounced away from me.

'Isn't Rosie confident and wonderful!' said Mum dreamily.

'No,' I said. 'And what was that about a lovers' tiff?'

'Well . . .' she said, 'I was looking at the pair of you yesterday and I suddenly thought, *wouldn't it be perfect if you were a little couple?*'

I honestly almost exploded. 'You want Rosie Taylor to be my *guuurgh* my *guuuurgh* . . .' I couldn't even bear to say the word. 'You want her to be my friend? Who's a girl? Have you gone totally nuts?'

'Wouldn't it be lovely?' said Mum.

'No. It'd be awful,' I replied. 'Tell her, Dad, please.'

But Dad was too busy jealously inspecting the surround-sound music system.

'Imagine,' said Mum, 'you two walking hand in hand on the beach outside their home in Barbados, while me and your father sip cocktails with her parents on the balcony.'

I couldn't believe my ears. 'I'd rather hold hands with a giant man-eating baby.'

Luckily, Rosie walked in at that moment. Trust me, that is not a sentence I ever thought I'd write but at least it shut Mum up.

Rosie switched on the TV, then fiddled around with the tablet.

'Maybe you two should sit together,' said Mum, pushing me towards Rosie.

For a split second, Rosie looked at me like she'd

found me floating in a public toilet. But then, a shy smile spread across her face. 'If you like.'

*What?!*

This was awful! I preferred it when Rosie hated me. Mum roughly shoved me down next to her.

After a few rings, Lee and Kat's faces appeared on the TV. Last time we'd spoken to them they'd been happy and excited. Now they looked tired and pale.

'What now?' said Lee flatly.

'Change of plan,' said Rosie.

Kat rubbed her eyes. 'But we already changed *everything*.'

'Just remember who's paying,' said Rosie's dad, coming in.

Lee and Kat looked like they were going to cry.

'Last night I had a setback,' said Rosie. 'I was beaten in a beauty contest by *that*.'

She pointed to Gamble, who was now dancing around in front of a mirror and punching himself in the face.

'So,' continued Rosie, 'I've decided our wedding needs to be even more special.'

'*Our* wedding?' asked Kat.

Rosie ignored her. 'I'll email you the new plans while we're driving. Roman's going to have a job too.'

*A job?*

My blood froze in my veins.

The only thing worse than being *at* a wedding is being *part* of the wedding. 'I don't want a j—'

'He'll do anything,' said Mum quickly.

'I thought so,' said Rosie, smiling like an evil octopus.

Lee screwed up his face. 'Look. This is too late and . . .'

'Tell someone who cares,' said Rosie, as she swept off down the motorhome. 'Mum. Dad. Roman's parents. You need to help me choose today's outfit.'

The adults all followed her and I was left alone in front of the TV.

'Roman!' begged Lee. 'Please help us.'

'How?'

'You've got to do something!' said Kat, practically weeping. 'You've got to save the wedding. Everyone else has gone mad.'

Lee and Kat looked at me desperately, but what on earth could *I* do? I gulped.

Luckily for me, everyone came back into the room and they hung up before Rosie could change the plans again.

Rosie's dad took the headphones back off

Gamble. I thought Gamble would have a full-on wig-out about this, like that time when our teacher Mrs McDonald told him he wasn't allowed to smoke a pipe in the classroom any more.

But he didn't.

In fact, I'd never seen him so calm and contented. He even listened attentively when Rosie's dad started showing off about his on-board gadgets. 'Watch this,' Rosie's dad said, jabbing the tablet.

'Good morning, Your Majesty,' came a robotic woman's voice from the speakers.

'Your Majesty?' said Dad.

'I programmed it to say that. Pretty good, eh?' Mr Taylor said. Dad ducked out of the way to avoid another shoulder slap. 'Right. We're going shopping, then we're going to Lakeview campsite off the motorway. Give us directions or I'll smash you to pieces!'

'Thank you, Your Majesty,' replied the computer voice. 'Calculating quickest route now.'

'Always does what I say,' said Rosie's dad, patting the tablet lovingly. 'When I threaten to smash the workers at my shopping centre to pieces, they cry like babies. Haha!'

We all pretended to smile. Apart from Gamble,

that is. He seemed to be deep in thought. This is unusual for him. The last time I saw him acting like this, I asked him what he was thinking about and he told me he was 'planning the best way to blow up a tortoise'.

A few minutes later we were back in our car, following Truckingham Palace along the main road.

'I'm glad he's got that SatNav,' said Dad, peering out through the sheets of rain. 'Otherwise we'd never find where we were going.'

'Exactly,' said Gamble.

I probably should've noticed something was wrong here, but I was more worried about a full day of shopping, Rosie's plans for me, and how on earth I was meant to save Lee and Kat's wedding.

As it turned out, I had far more immediate problems to worry about.

## Shopping

After about three hours of driving, Dad parked up in a large car park in a town centre. We climbed out and sploshed through the puddles to Truckingham Palace.

Vanya filmed as Rosie thrust a piece of paper into each of our hands. 'This is a map of all the shops in the town, and a plan of how long we'll spend in each one.'

'Why haven't I got a map? 'Snot fair,' said Gamble, sticking out his bottom lip.

Rosie tried a sweet smile, but this made her look like a murderous gerbil. 'I thought we could tie you up outside the shops, like a dog.'

Gamble looked as if he was going to cry.

He did have a point there – it *was* pretty mean. But then again, Rosie had a point too. The last time I went into a clothes shop with Gamble, he stole a pair of knickers and used them as a catapult to fire stink bombs at old ladies.

'Why can't I just stay in here and listen to Smash Fest?' he asked. 'The Hairy Toddlers are playing.'

'Er . . . because you're a disgustamungous reject and we'd have to have the whole place fumigated afterwards,' replied Rosie.

'I won't bust anything, promise,' whined Gamble.

Rosie's dad stroked his chin. 'At least he won't be able to shoplift if he stays here. We can put him in the garage.'

'Hmm,' said Rosie, 'it's a bit like a prison cell. He'll feel right at home.'

'We'll get the sports car out first, of course,' said

her dad, 'and everything can be voice-activated from down there so we won't even need to give him the tablet.'

'Perfect!' said Gamble.

So, leaving him behind, we trudged off through the storm and into town.

I don't want to go into detail about what happened next. Let's just say it was the most boring afternoon of my life. Mum and Mrs Taylor went off 'for some pampering'. The rest of us followed Rosie.

We all had to stand about in these really posh, expensive shops while she tried on endless piles of horrible clothes. Each time, she'd strut out of the changing rooms and say something like: 'I know I look incredible, but is it going to change the world?'

Even though I was still mad at Vanya, I felt a little bit sorry for her. She had to film Rosie on an iPad as a live webcast. Amazingly, thousands of pathetic, sad people across the globe were actually watching Rosie shopping, and sending messages to tell her what they thought of the outfits. Things like:

OMG hun. You look amazetastic in that blue dress! (She didn't by the way – she looked like a badly wrapped birthday present).

Or:

Go girl. Ur gonna make people puke with jealousy when they see you @ that wedding! (I actually agreed with that one, apart from the words 'with jealousy.')

But the worst one was:

U look gorgeamungous but who's the weird little mutant in the background? (I realised that this was aimed at me. *Charming!*)

After that nasty comment, Vanya switched off the iPad and just pretended to film from then on. Even though I was still cross with her, it *was* a nice thing to do. In fact, I almost said thank-you.

Believe it or not, this was actually the highlight of the day.

My mum and Rosie's mum met us after their 'very expensive' haircuts, which didn't seem to have made any difference at all. Then Rosie told my mum that she wanted to buy me a special present, and could I take all of the shopping bags back to Truckingham Palace for her while she bought it?

*A present?* I didn't like the sound of this at all. But before I could say no, Mum said, 'A gentleman will do anything for his lady love.'

I nearly hurled.

When we finally got back, I dumped the bags inside the motorhome and we let Gamble out of the garage. He was bouncing about everywhere. 'That was amazing! The Hairy Toddlers played all their classics.'

I massaged my blistered hands. 'Classics?'

'Yeah. You know, like "Setting Fire to People is Fun" and "Kick Me in the Head if You Love Me".'

'Right,' I said.

'Well, I'd love to have you all inside Truckingham Palace to wait for Rosie,' said Rosie's dad, 'but I'm going to have a nap before we set off. They could be some time . . .'

They were, as well. In fact, we were waiting in the car for two whole hours. Dad tried to have a snooze too, but he couldn't because Gamble wouldn't shut up about The Hairy Toddlers. To keep him quiet, we had to put Radio Brain Smash on the stereo and stuff tissues into our ears. Outside, the rain became even heavier, hammering onto the roof of the car.

Finally, Vanya, Rosie and her mum pulled up in a taxi, bringing two more huge bags.

When Rosie walked past our car, Mum wound the window down. 'Did you get everything you needed?'

'Yes, thank you, Mrs G,' she simpered. 'Including my little present for Roman.'

'Oooh! How exciting!' said Mum, clapping her hands together. 'And romantic.'

'Gross,' I said.

'I'll give it to you tomorrow,' sniggered Rosie. 'Now let's go. Lakeview Campsite, here we come!'

Still laughing, she swept off back to Truckingham Palace. Vanya smiled weakly at me, then followed her.

The last time I heard Rosie laugh like that was after a school swimming lesson, when she'd sneaked into the boys' changing room and cut the bottom out of my trousers with a pair of scissors.

Dad was tired, so Mum drove, slowly following Truckingham Palace through the torrential rain and out of the car park.

'Off to another expensive campsite,' grumbled Dad.

'It's gonna be awesome!' said Gamble.

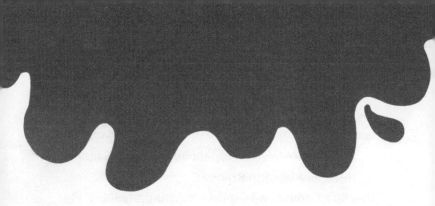

# Afternoon and Evening

## The SatNav Lets Us Down and Gamble Makes New Friends

It's easy to look back now and say we should've known better. There *were* plenty of clues along the way:

Clue 1: Dad kept checking the map and saying things like, 'This can't be right. We're going *away* from the campsite.' Mum was convinced that Mr Taylor's SatNav was taking us on a special route to avoid the traffic.

Clue 2: The campsite was meant to be near the motorway. But, when we finally came off the motorway, we drove for ages down narrow, winding country lanes into the middle of nowhere.

Clue 3: Gamble was quiet. He's only quiet when he's hiding something. Like when he locked that Year Two kid in a cupboard to see if he could 'make a skeleton'.

Clue 4: The people. At first there were just a couple – dressed in black, covered in tattoos and walking along the side of the lane. But gradually, there were more and more of them, all heading in the same direction. Some were carrying tents; others had rucksacks on their backs.

Clue 5: The massive traffic jam we got stuck in. 'Must be sheep ahead,' said Mum, but she didn't sound convinced. By now it was clear something was wrong. Gamble was clapping his hands together and saying, 'Getting close!'

Dad finally asked Mum to turn the car around. But she couldn't. The road was only just wide enough for one vehicle. We were tight behind Truckingham Palace, and another car (a scruffy wreck with 'The Death Machine' scrawled on the bonnet) was right up behind our bumper.

Yes, we were stupid to ignore the clues. And before we knew it, it was too late.

Eventually, we crawled around a tight bend. A sign was nailed to a tree. On it was an arrow pointing through a gate and the word 'campsite' sprayed in black paint. There was also a skull and crossbones on the sign, but nobody seemed to notice that except me. The cars in front slowly followed the arrow through the gate.

'We're here!' said Mum triumphantly, as Truckingham Palace turned off the road. 'I told you to trust his SatNav. It's voice-activated, you know.'

'Hmm,' said Dad. 'I was expecting something a bit smarter.'

Mum tutted. 'It must be a good site if the Taylors chose it. I hope there's room for us.'

Unfortunately, this would be the least of our worries.

A girl with pink hair waved us into a muddy field. She had about three hundred earrings in each ear and black lipstick. Mum wound down the window. 'Would it be possible to stay near to the tropical swimming paradise?'

The girl put her finger into one of her nostrils and snotted out the other one all over our windscreen. 'Park over there, where you're told,' she grunted.

Mum wound the window up. 'I don't think much of their customer service.'

She inched forward through the rain, the wheels skidding and the caravan sliding about behind us. We parked next to Truckingham Palace at the end of a row of cars. A few people were putting up tents on tiny patches of mud.

'This must be wrong,' said Dad.

'Rosie's dad is a man of style and taste,' replied Mum. 'He wouldn't take us somewhere that wasn't perfect.'

Sadly, she was very wrong about that.

Rosie's dad climbed out of Truckingham Palace and squelched over to our car, looking flustered. 'I've a good mind to complain to the manager. It's nothing like the pictures on the website. And as for the *people*? You pay top dollar to avoid scrut-bags like these.'

He nodded towards a man with no top on, who was walking past with a massive lizard perched on his shoulder.

'Maybe the SatNav got it wrong?' Dad offered.

Rosie's dad scoffed. 'Rubbish. It's worth more than your car. As long as you tell it where to go it's never . . .'

His voice trailed away. Very slowly we all turned towards Gamble, who was looking out of the window, whistling innocently. And it was then that I noticed what was written on the back of his hand. Those letters and numbers he'd been writing there for the past two days. What were they? A code? A password? Or . . .

I remembered something that the Radio Brain Smash DJ had said yesterday. 'Is that a *postcode*, Darren?' I asked, grabbing his wrist. Everything suddenly made sense.

He pulled his hand away and licked the back of it to get rid of the pen marks. 'Can't prove nothing.'

Rosie's dad's face went a funny shade of purple. 'Did you talk to my SatNav when we were shopping?'

'Course not. Can't prove nothing.'

'You did. YOU programmed it to take us here! Where *are* we, you little b—'

He was drowned out by a loud scream, followed by a shuddering BOOM BOOM BOOM that shook the car and thudded right through my chest. It seemed to be coming from behind a thick hedge at the end of the field.

From nowhere, a couple of people bundled past Rosie's dad. And they weren't alone. Hundreds were stampeding from every direction like a herd of tattooed zebras in leather trousers.

All of them were charging towards a gate halfway down the hedge. When they got there, they fought each other to scramble over it.

'What the . . . ?' I said.

THUD THUD THUD! PEEEEOOOOOOOO WWWW! came the deafening noise again.

'GOOOOD EVENING, SMAAAASHHH FEST!' said a loud echoing voice from behind the trees, followed by a great cheer.

*Smash Fest?!*

Of course!

When we went shopping, we'd left Gamble inside Truckingham Palace with a voice-activated SatNav. How could we have been so foolish?

'Sweaty Sue and The Armpits are onstage!' Gamble said, hopping out onto the muddy ground and shoving past Rosie, who'd stormed out of the motorhome to see what was going on. 'Don't wait up for me!'

Before we could stop him, he sprinted off. There was a brief moment when we could see him running across the roof of someone's car. But then he hopped down off the bonnet and disappeared into the crowd.

Mum panicked. 'What are we going to do? We're meant to be looking after him.'

'Hashtag: leave him,' said Rosie, like this was the most obvious thing in the world. 'I'm not staying here. He's happy with all the other scuzzbuckets. He can eat mud and go to the toilet in his pants. He'll love it.'

Mum seemed too worried about Darren to notice Rosie being horrible.

Rosie's dad sniffed. 'She's got a point. We should get going – we passed a five-star luxury hotel two miles back.'

'But . . .' said Mum. Rosie and her dad ignored her and skidded back through the mud to Truckingham Palace.

The whole world seemed to shake as the thumping, squealing, deafening music started again.

Mum turned to Dad. 'You'll have to go and find him.'

'*Me?*' cried Dad. 'Have you *seen* those people?'

'What if something happens to him?' asked Mum. 'We'll never forgive ourselves.'

Sighing, Dad reached for the door.

## My First Music Festival

I'm not sure why I went after Dad. I guess I felt like I just *had* to help him. Gamble might be a stick-insect-murdering nutcase who once forced me to eat an entire Pritt Stick 'for a laugh'. But he's still my friend.

Sort of.

'You should've stayed in the car,' said Dad, as I skidded alongside him. 'We've no idea what might be behind that hedge.'

The music was getting louder, if that was possible – a howling explosion of sound that made my teeth throb.

The gate had been trampled to the ground and we had to keep our eyes on our feet as we picked our way over it. Dad held my hand to support me. 'Hopefully we'll find h . . . *oh my word*!'

I looked up and stopped in my tracks. We were facing what could only be described as a riot. Thousands of people were leaping around the muddy field, crashing into each other in a mad, tangled scrum. Glasses and bottles were being hurled from all parts of the crowd, falling like bombs in the rain.

I'd never been to a music festival before. And I'm now pretty sure I never want to go to one again.

At the far end of the field was a stage, which was really just a lorry trailer with one side rolled up. Towering skyscrapers of speakers stood either side of it, booming out noise. And at the back of the stage, a long-haired, topless drummer was smashing away at his drum kit. When one of the sticks snapped, he just started attacking the drums with his bare hands.

There were three other people up there with him. One woman (who I guessed from the dark stains on her vest was Sweaty Sue) and two other men (the rest of The Armpits). They seemed to be having an actual fight with each other. The 'music' came from the guitarist hitting the bass player round the head with his guitar, while Sweaty Sue dangled off his neck, screaming into the microphone.

She then used the microphone lead to strangle the bass player, who carried on playing even as he fell to his knees. As his eyes began to bulge, the guitarist karate-kicked them both offstage, and they disappeared into the crowd. Meanwhile, the drummer had given up trying to play the drums and was now throwing them at the crowd. Unbelievably, the wailing guitars and shouting continued.

And, even more unbelievably, the audience loved it.

We were just beginning to edge backwards when Dad pointed towards the stage.

The unmistakable figure of Darren Gamble had scrambled up there. He raised his arms to the audience and grabbed a spare microphone. It screeched with feedback. 'Make some noise if you're a filthy ratbag!' he yelled.

The crowd went crazy, screaming and surging towards him. Then Gamble ran to the front of the stage and dived off the edge of it. For a few moments he was tossed up and down like a skinny beach ball, before being swallowed up by the tangled mass of bodies.

'They'll tear his arms and legs off,' I said.

'We should go back to the car . . .' said Dad. Then, after a few seconds, he quickly added, 'And get help.'

But then a fresh group of people burst through the gate. Before we knew it, we were being pushed forward.

'Help!' I cried, frantically reaching for Dad's arm as we were separated and jostled towards the crowd.

'Roooo-mannn!' he called.

I was shoved, dragged and swept away. All I could see were arms and chests. Bodies were bashing into me, spinning me round and round, almost knocking me over. I fought to stay upright and I tried to scream but the air was squeezed from my lungs. And the music kept on pumping out. A woman was being passed over everyone's heads, and her boot caught my shoulder. The person next to me pulled her down and slammed her face first onto the ground. She fought her way to her feet, then grabbed me by the ears and screamed, 'THIS IS AMAZING!' before bouncing off into the crowd.

By now I was seriously scared. I could hardly breathe because of the crush and the smell of wet, sweaty leather. My legs felt like they were going to give way any second. I grasped at the people around me but I felt myself slipping and sinking towards the muddy ground.

And then, just as my knees began to buckle, someone slapped me on the top of my head. 'ROMAN!'

## Saved

I looked up and my heart nearly exploded.

*Vanya!*

She was surfing across the top of the crowd, held up by their hands. I reached up and she grabbed my wrist and hauled me towards her. She couldn't do it by herself though – I had to climb up the arms and legs of an enormous man with tattoos all over him.

'Get off!' he growled, then launched me upwards. Before I knew it I was on top of the crowd, being thrown around.

By this point, Sweaty Sue and The Armpits had clambered back onstage. The drummer was playing his one remaining drum by headbutting it next to a microphone, while Sweaty Sue set fire to the unconscious guitarist's shoes (while he was still wearing them) and screamed something about eating her own brain.

'We've gotta get out of here!' yelled Vanya, helping me to stagger to my feet. We were literally standing on people's heads and shoulders. 'Run for it!'

So we stumbled towards the back of the crowd, objects being hurled at us the whole way. Now and then our feet would disappear into a gap between bodies and we'd have to pull ourselves back up. Some people helped us. Others tried to drag us down or knock us over. But somehow we struggled to the back, where we dropped to the ground and staggered to the edge of the field.

'Thank you!' I panted, checking my bruises.

'I followed you into the field and, when you disappeared, I thought . . .'

For a few moments we didn't say anything. Various blood-soaked, mud-covered weirdoes were bumbling around us looking dazed. On the stage, Sweaty Sue had now also set fire to her own hair, and was running around like a flaming torch.

'I guess I won't be booking them to play at my nan's birthday party,' said Vanya. I smiled and she took a deep breath. 'Look. I'm really sorry I came away with Rosie and not with you.'

'Huh,' I said, suddenly cross again.

'I didn't know how to tell you. I didn't even want to come with Rosie at all. But I really want to make films when I'm older. And she said I could film her and she'd buy me a camera and everything.'

'You lied to me . . . for a free camera.'

'No! My mum had already told Rosie's parents I'd love to go. She thought it'd be a great experience. And she wants me to meet new friends. I know it was so stupid – I'm really sorry, Roman. I tried to argue with Mum but she wasn't having any of it. She told me she'd be humiliated if I suddenly told Rosie I wasn't going.'

Something softened slightly inside me. 'Well, my mum wants me to *marry* Rosie.'

Vanya pulled a face. 'Gross. She's been a complete nightmare. All she ever talks about is how gorgeous and amazing she is. This morning I had to film her practising her song for the wedding.'

'Was she any good?' I asked, a smile building on my lips because I already knew the answer.

'She sounded like a car crashing through a shop window.'

I giggled. I still thought Vanya was brilliant, even if she had gone behind my back.

'Let's get back,' she said, standing up and pulling me to my feet. 'Friends?'

I smiled, and we squelched off back to the car.

## Where Have You Been?

We found Dad looking shaken next to the gate. He was holding a hanky underneath his bleeding nose. 'You're safe!' he said, hugging me. 'I was so worried. Any luck finding Darren?'

I slapped my forehead. *Gamble!*

I felt really guilty. I'd been so concerned about myself that I'd completely forgotten about him.

'Maybe we should check back at the car before we go out there again?' suggested Vanya.

This seemed like a good idea. But when we got back, Rosie Taylor was blocking our path with her hands on her hips and her face like thunder. 'Where have you been?'

Dad cleared his throat. 'We were just look—'

'I wasn't talking to you, Franken-freak's Father,' she snapped. 'I was talking to my so-called friend. Apparently we can't leave here without you, Vanya, and I've had to wait for an hour while a whole host of flea-ridden scumbags traipse past me.'

The engine of Truckingham Palace roared into life and Rosie's dad called out from his window, 'Come on, girls! We're getting out of here right now.'

'Sorry for saving Roman,' said Vanya sarcastically.

'Not as sorry as I am,' Rosie snapped. 'You are here to make me happy and film me. Nothing else. And now I find you're hanging round with this marshmallow-brained undie-sniffer.'

*Lovely.*

Vanya raised her eyebrows. 'Don't speak to Roman like that.'

It was nice of her to stand up for me. I felt like I was getting my friend back.

The engine of the motorhome revved. 'I'll just turn her round while you're having your little chat,' called Rosie's dad.

'Vanya, I command you never to speak to Roman again.'

'I'll talk to who I want,' replied Vanya coolly.

'Yeah? Well, you can *stay* with him too because you're no longer welcome in Truckingham Palace. Hashtag: banned.'

I could tell that Vanya was about to yell back at Rosie, but then something brilliant happened.

The engine revved hard. The wheels spun. But

the coach didn't move. And a massive jet of mud sprayed up from the tyres and soaked Rosie from head to toe.

For a moment she just stood there, completely covered in sticky brown filth. But then she howled, 'Daddy, you complete monkey-armpit! You've ruined my outfit!'

Vanya looked at her, completely innocent. 'Would you like me to film *this* as well, Rosie?'

Rosie stomped off, and Vanya and I grinned at each other.

## Bad Things and Good Things

Some bad things and some good things happened next.

- **Bad thing**: Truckingham Palace was completely stuck in the mud.
- **Good thing**: Rosie demanded that her dad call the AA to tow them out immediately.
- **Bad thing**: The AA couldn't reach us. Apparently, soon after we'd arrived, someone had chopped down a load of trees to block the road so that the police couldn't get in and stop the festival.

- **Good thing:** Furious, Rosie used her dad's credit card to order a helicopter to pick them up and take them back to the hotel.
- **Bad thing:** When the helicopter landed in the field, a bunch of nutters tried to smash it up. Some of them even picked up a portable toilet and charged at the helicopter, holding up the loo like a battering ram.
- **Good thing:** Vanya had refused to go. She'd said that, since Gamble was lost, she should stay with me.
- **Amazing thing:** Just before he climbed into the helicopter, Rosie's dad tossed my dad the keys to Truckingham Palace and told him to 'guard it with his life' and not let any of 'these long-haired low-lifes anywhere near it!'

'You are kidding me!' Rosie had screamed, pointing at me. 'I wouldn't even leave that useless butt sponge in charge of a tricycle.'

*Butt sponge.*

She was only being horrible because my mum was out of earshot.

'They're more likely to keep it safe if they're inside it,' said her dad. 'Their lives will depend on it.'

'Hmmm . . .' said Rosie. 'So if it *does* get damaged, at least Roman will get damaged too.'

'I *am* here,' I said.

She didn't hear us because the helicopter engine had roared into life and the propellers had begun to spin. Soon they were taking off, with Rosie literally stamping on the fingers of the loonies who were hanging onto the landing skids.

Of course we moved in straight away. Mum told us to be mega-careful. 'Let's keep it perfect for them. Then next time they'll trust us with one of their holiday homes.'

I have to say it was amazing in there – almost completely soundproof from the racket outside and a million times cleaner and better than the crudmobile we'd slept in the night before. Vanya, Dad and I sat on the sofa and watched TV, while Mum went out on another Gamble hunt.

After about an hour, she came back, deathly white. Her glasses were missing, her clothes were ripped and there was spit all over her back.

'Are you all right?' asked Dad.

She took a deep breath. 'Well, I asked two people if they knew where the lost children's tent was . . .'

'And?' I asked.

'The first one laughed and said, "What kind of an idiot would bring kids here?"'

'Makes sense,' said Dad.

'And the other one said: "Try the black tent at the end. It's where they're doing the animal sacrifices."'

'Oh,' I said, trying not to imagine Gamble being sliced up on an altar.

Dad made her a cup of tea but her hands were shaking so much it sploshed everywhere. 'I saw Darren in the end though.'

*What a relief!* 'Is he OK?'

'He's fine. He was with a motorcycle gang.'

'How do you know they were a motorcycle gang?' said Dad, mopping up her tea spill.

'There were a gang of them,' said Mum, 'and they all had motorbikes.'

'Of course.'

Mum sniffed. 'Darren looked happy. He was riding on the back of someone's bike. You should've heard him laughing as it ploughed through a crowd of people . . .'

'Sounds like Gamble,' I said.

'What was the gang called?' asked Dad.

'Well, they all had jackets with "The Scummy

Snot-Flickers" written on them,' said Mum. 'Darren was wearing one of their leather waistcoats. And I'm pretty sure he'd had a tattoo done.'

Trust Gamble to join up with people like that.

'And what happened to you?' I asked.

'Darren was just telling me he'd be back later and not to worry about him when I got dragged off into the crowd. It was . . . *terrible*. There was a band onstage called The Head Stompers. Whatever you do, don't make me go back out there. *Please!*'

She was clinging to my sleeve and her eyes were wild with fear.

Eventually, Mum and Dad decided to ring Gamble's mum, putting the mobile on speakerphone. It rang three times, then she picked it up.

'What do you want?' came a gruff voice from the other end. I'd never heard Gamble's mum before. She sounded like a walrus with a sore throat.

'It's . . . er . . . Darren,' said Mum.

'You don't sound like Darren . . .' replied Gamble's mum. 'Is this a wind-up? Cos if it is I'll knock your teeth so far down your throat you'll be chewin' your toenails.'

'No. It's Roman's mum. We're *worried* about Darren.'

'What's he done now?' growled Gamble's mum. 'He's not been going to the bog in people's shoes again, has he? Filthy little grub. I keep telling him: do it in a toilet. Or someone's garden. Or a bus shelter. Amount of times I've put my foot in my slippers an—'

'No,' interrupted Mum, 'he's lost.'

'Lost?'

'At a music festival. He disappeared and . . .' her voice trailed away.

There was a long pause. I thought Gamble's mum was going to go mental at us but she just said, 'Oh. That all? He's always running off somewhere but he always comes back. He's like a boomerang. Unfortunately. Ha! Now, if you don't mind, I've just knocked over a fox in my car and it ain't gonna cook itself.'

With that, she hung up.

'We'll just have to wait then,' said Dad. 'Unless anyone wants to go back out there and look for him . . .'

We all suddenly found the floor to be really, really interesting.

## The After Party

Two hours later, it was getting dark outside and Gamble still hadn't turned up. We were watching monster truck racing on TV, when . . .

THUNK!

'What was that?' I said.

Dad muted the TV.

For a moment there was total silence from outside. Then . . .

THUNK THUNK THUNK!

It was coming from right above our heads. But what *was* it? Giant seagulls? An alien spacecraft?

THUNK    THUNK    THUNK    THUNK **BOOOOOOOM!**

'What's going on?' said Mum, her voice quivering.

And then it happened.

There was a terrible sound of wrenching metal from above. Then a pair of legs burst through the roof.

A pair of legs!

Through the roof!

They dangled there, waggling around wildly before disappearing, leaving a massive hole behind them.

Dad ran to the door, flung it open and stopped dead in his tracks. There were thousands – and I mean *thousands* – of people outside the motorhome, packed into the field like sardines and staring right at us. He slammed it shut again. 'We're under attack!'

Gamble's head popped down through the hole in the ceiling. 'All right?' he chirped. Since the last time I'd seen him, he'd painted his scalp green and there was a snake tattoo stretching all the way up his arm.

'What's going on?' asked Mum.

Outside, the crowd had started to chant: '*Music – music – music.*'

'The speakers blew up onstage,' said Gamble. 'Music too loud, see. So I brought the party back here. We can hook the bands up to the sound system, innit.'

'But what's all the noise from up there? And whose were those legs?' said Mum.

'Oh, that's just the drummer from The Cheesy Toenails. They're setting up on the roof,' said Gamble cheerfully.

'Awfully sorry,' came a surprisingly polite voice from somewhere above us.

'Pass us the control tablet, Roman,' said Gamble.

Too shocked not to obey, I found it and passed it up to him.

'And plug this in while you're at it,' he continued, holding a wire down towards me. 'The sound guy says there should be a socket somewhere on the sound system.'

I did as he asked.

'Wicked!' said Gamble, pulling himself back up through the hole. 'ONE TWO THREE FOUR!'

Then the noise hit us.

It poured in through the hole in the roof like a flock of evil bats. And no matter how hard I jammed my fingers into my ears, I couldn't escape it. It surrounded me. I fell to my knees as it rattled my ribcage and slapped my brain.

Dad staggered across the room and yanked the cord out of the wall.

The music immediately stopped, apart from the drums, which banged a few more times before they died off too. My skull felt like it had just been released from a headlock and my ears were ringing.

But things got suddenly worse.

It started with a loud booing. Then objects began smacking against the motorhome. Gamble's head appeared through the hole in the roof, yelling at us to plug the speakers back in before there was a riot.

It was too late though.

Because Truckingham Palace had started to move.

At first it was a gentle swaying, but it soon built up until the whole motorhome was tipping from one side to another like a tiny boat in a storm. Outside, the crowd were pressing towards us, chanting, 'Tip it! Tip it!' as we were flung from one side of the lounge to the other.

Clinging to the furniture to keep himself upright, Dad stumbled to the door and almost fell outside. 'Please stop!' he begged the crowd.

This had mixed results.

On the plus side, the crowd stopped rocking us. But, when they let go, Truckingham Palace slammed into the ground with a loud *CRUNCH*, sending Dad flying across the room.

'That did *not* sound good,' said Vanya.

It didn't *look* good either. There was a jagged crack in the floor, leading from one side of the motorhome to the other. It was so wide you could've posted a doughnut through it.

'They'll never invite us on holiday again!' exclaimed Mum.

But there wasn't time to celebrate because, at that moment, the crowd surged towards the open door.

'Quick!' shouted Dad, grabbing me and Vanya. 'Down here!'

Luckily, the first few people all tried to push through at the same time. They got stuck in the doorway, giving us just enough time to leg it across the lounge and through the kitchen, before diving into one of the spare rooms and locking the door behind us.

On the other side of the door we could hear absolute chaos. The crowd had forced its way inside. There were hundreds of pounding footsteps. People were shouting and fighting. Glass was smashed. Furniture was wrenched from the walls. Music was pumping out of the speakers again. Bodies were flung against doors. And, from somewhere, what sounded like a motorbike engine was being revved.

With all this going on, we cowered in terror among all of Rosie's spare clothes.

'There's nowhere to go!' wailed Mum from by the window. 'We're surrounded.'

'If we don't get out of this alive,' said Dad,

leaning against the door as someone on the other side attempted to kick it in, 'I want you all to know that it's been great knowing you.'

The kicks got harder. The door began to strain against its hinges. There was a sound of splintering wood. We all closed our eyes and tensed our bodies and then . . .

## Flashing Lights

Suddenly it stopped.

Just like that.

It was as though a wizard had clicked his fingers and made everyone disappear. We could hear people jostling and shoving towards the exit.

And then there was silence.

After a few minutes, I cautiously opened the door.

'Chicken-flavoured doughnuts!' I shrieked.

A fire was burning in the lounge. Seriously! Someone had smashed up every single piece of furniture in the whole motorhome and set it alight in the middle of the carpet.

'Don't panic!' yelled Dad, completely panicking and flapping about for a fire extinguisher.

From through the hole in the roof, I noticed a

single stream of liquid raining down on the burning wood.

*What the . . . ?* I thought, squinting upwards.

'I've got this,' called Gamble, from the roof.

It took me a moment to realise where the liquid was coming from.

'Oh, gross!' I said, covering my eyes.

Gamble was trying to *wee* out the flames.

'Glad I drank that four-litre bottle of Coke!' he said, gushing away like a disgusting garden hose.

It was only when he finally stopped and the flames sizzled out that we were able to look around at the damage.

The place was wrecked.

As well as the hole in the ceiling, the burnt carpet and the crack in the floor, the walls were black from the smoke. Every single window had been smashed, and the TV and sound system had both been stolen. Shards of broken glass and splintered wood littered the floor.

'Where did everyone go?' asked Vanya behind me.

Until then, I hadn't thought about this. But then I noticed the flashing blue lights outside.

Three policemen in full riot gear burst in, wielding truncheons and plastic shields.

'GETONTHEFLOORANDDON'TMOVE!' one of them yelled.

Terrified, we all dived to the ground. 'Please don't break my face!' I cried.

'This your motorhome?' said the riot policeman.

'No,' said Dad.

'So you nicked it?'

'No . . . well . . . we *borrowed* it and—'

The policeman was interrupted by Gamble, who swung down through the hole in the roof screaming, 'Ninja Gamble to the rescue!' and trying to elbow-drop him. Sadly he missed and landed face first on the ground. 'Brutal,' he groaned.

## They'll Never Notice

The police officers soon realised we weren't violent rioters. They told us that we'd been seriously lucky that they'd got there in time to scare off the crowd. For about three hours, they'd been trying to get onto the site. They'd just removed the last tree trunk from the road in time to save us. Ten more seconds and we'd have been toast.

Outside, the festival was over. Most of the nutters had scattered, and half of the cars had already driven off the site. A few people were being dragged into police vans. Others were standing about in small groups, shouting nasty things at the police, then running away when they got near.

'Why did the police have to ruin the party?' said Gamble, twitching angrily. 'It was just getting good.'

I slapped my hand over my eyes.

'What are we going to tell the Taylors?' asked Mum.

Gamble sniffed. 'Don't tell 'em nothing. It's the Gamble family motto. They'll never notice.'

'Darren,' I said, 'you can see the moon through the roof. And I think they might just notice the motorbike in the Jacuzzi.'

'Nyaa,' said Gamble, waving my words away like they were wasps. 'We can tidy it up in no time.'

'How are you going to tidy up the fire?' said Vanya. 'Or the crack in the floor? Or the fridge? Someone put a live goat in it.'

'They were just having a laugh,' said Gamble.

Biting her lip, Mum took out her phone, nervously jabbed at the screen, then held it to her ear. It seemed to ring for a very long time before she finally spoke. 'I'm sorry to wake you. It's about your motorhome . . .'

# SUNDAY

# Rosie's Family Take Things Pretty Well

We all went back to our caravan to try and get some rest before the Taylors arrived. On the phone Mum had just said that there'd been 'a bit of a problem' and Rosie's dad 'might like to have a look'.

This was like a doctor telling someone who'd just had their leg bitten off by a lion that they'd 'had a little scratch'.

He said he'd come first thing in the morning because Rosie had said that, 'If anyone disturbs my beauty sleep, I'll have them turned into marmalade, spread onto scones and fed to a bunch of hungry old people.'

She's nice like that.

Vanya, Dad and I napped in our mouldy old caravan because, unbelievably, it was much nicer than Truckingham Palace. Gamble didn't go to bed. Instead he spent the whole night hanging out with The Cheesy Toenails. For some reason, Mum did her best to tidy and clean the smouldering, shattered remains of Truckingham Palace. This was a total waste of time and was never going to get rid of all the filth. A bit like Gamble having a shower.

The Taylors arrived the next morning in a taxi, just as we were waking up. When they saw the state of Truckingham Palace, they took it pretty well.

OK, so by 'took it pretty well' I mean that they freaked out and went totally nuts.

Rosie's dad cried his eyes out. It was quite embarrassing really. At one point, when he was lying on his front, beating the floor with his fists, he said he loved Truckingham Palace more than he loved Rosie. Even though he later took this back, I could definitely see why. I mean, Truckingham

Palace wasn't annoying or horrible at all. And you can't even watch regular TV on Rosie, let alone satellite.

Rosie's mum seemed more concerned about where they were going to stay that night. 'Get up off the floor and call the insurance company,' she snapped at Rosie's dad. 'You'd better have a replacement here in an hour.'

Meanwhile, Rosie concentrated all her anger on us. 'I told Dad not to leave this family of slop-brained pigs' anuses in charge,' she roared at her mum. 'What do you expect from people who could live with Roman for eleven years and *not* float him out to sea on his own in a small basket?'

'It's not Roman's fault,' said Vanya, but Rosie ignored her.

'At least I took the wedding outfits with me.'

'Steady on,' said Dad. 'There were about three thousand people here. What could we do?'

Rosie flicked back her hair. 'Well – *duh* – if they were desperate to destroy something, I'd have tossed Roman out to them. They could've torn him limb from limb. It might've at least saved the carpets.'

'I *am* here,' I said.

'Darling,' whispered Rosie's mum, loud enough

for us to hear. 'Don't worry about these frightful people. Once your father's done on the phone, we'll have a replacement motorhome, then we'll be rid of them for good.' She turned to my dad. 'No offence of course.'

'None taken,' said Dad, rolling his eyes.

At that moment, Mum came out of Truckingham Palace. Her hands were red-raw from scrubbing the motorhome all night and she had black rings round her eyes. 'We're so sorry,' she croaked.

'Well, it's not good enough!' snarled Rosie's mum.

Mum's mouth opened and closed a few times like a lost fish as Rosie's mum carried on ranting. 'And if you think you're ever coming on holiday with us again . . .'

*No more holidays with Rosie!* I hadn't been this excited since Dad brought home that twenty-four-pack of slightly-out-of-date Squidgy Splodge doughnuts last month.

But then something really weird happened

'Don't worry, Mrs Garstang,' said Rosie, stepping in front of her mum. 'We all make mistakes.'

I didn't like the way she looked at me as she said this.

Rosie continued. 'Mummy's just upset, but it's OK. We'll still have a great time with you at the wedding. And we're such good friends now that we're sure to have more holidays in the future.'

'But you just said . . .' I began

Rosie waved me away. 'We can't let a teeny-weeny bit of damage get in the way of a friendship, can we? I mean, Roman and I have got such an important job to do together at the wedding . . .'

Then she did something utterly horrible. She put her arm round me. Honestly. Her arm. It was horrible, like being hugged by a rotten cucumber. Mum clasped her hands over her heart and made an *awwww* sound, as if she'd just seen a baby cuddling a puppy or something.

Meanwhile, Mr Taylor was seriously losing his rag down the phone. 'What do you mean, I'm *not insured*?' he was yelling, furious with the person at the other end of the phone. 'But that's what *being insured* means – if the motorhome gets smashed up, you get me a new one . . . No, you moron, I don't know *who* smashed it up. I wasn't here . . . yes I did leave it unlocked but . . . well, *I* didn't know it was an illegal music festival. If I did, I wouldn't have gone to it . . . but how is it *my* fault?'

He angrily jabbed his phone to end the call.

'And . . .' said Rosie's mum.

Rosie's dad cleared his throat. 'Well, we'll just have to stay in a hotel tonight. We've still got the car. It'll be fine.'

He called a hotel. At first he was perfectly calm, answering questions and being polite. But soon he was angry again. 'There's *got* to be money in my bank account!' he roared. 'I'm completely loaded. Don't you know who I am?'

'What's happening, Daddy?' asked Rosie.

He looked at his phone in disbelief. 'Hung up on me!'

There followed a third phone call, which he made inside the ruins of the motorhome. Afterwards he called Rosie and her mum inside to talk. It was obvious that something serious was happening.

When Rosie's parents trooped out again a few minutes later, her dad had sagged like a deflated balloon. Her mum had a great big cheesy grin fixed across her face.

'Hi!' she gushed at Mum. 'Wasn't it funny how we just had that silly little fallout?'

Mum narrowed her eyes. 'Hilarious.'

Rosie's mum was still grinning. 'So we were all

thinking. Wouldn't it be so cute if we all stayed with you tonight?'

'You weren't very nice to me,' said Mum.

'But that was before we needed to borrow money off you,' said Rosie's mum, as though this made it all right.

'Borrow money? Off us?' asked Dad.

'There's been a bit of a problem,' said Rosie's dad, rubbing the back of his neck. 'I've . . . er . . . run out of cash.'

'I thought you were rolling in it,' said Dad.

Rosie's dad gulped. 'Well, I was, but then I paid for the motorhome, and the helicopter and the shopping spree . . . it all added up. The bank have frozen my account until I get paid next month.'

Just then, Rosie staggered out of the caravan, crying her eyes out. She was filming herself with her phone on a selfie stick. 'OMG, fans! Welcome to a sad day on Rosie-dot-TV. This is soooooo awfulatious!' she snivelled. 'My dream of starring at my very own wedding has been ruined. Ruined! All I ever wanted was for you to love me! But now I've got to go home. Boohoo.'

I looked at Vanya, who rolled her eyes. Rosie was obviously faking it.

Mum totally believed her though. 'Oh, don't cry, Rosie,' she said.

'This is the only person in the world who can save my big day,' Rosie said, before turning the stick round to point at my mum.

Mum gulped. 'Well . . . I . . . er . . .'

'All you've got to do is let us stay in your sweet little caravan, then Roman and I can be together at this wedding.'

'Stay in *that* disgusting turd bucket? Have you gone mad?' cried Rosie's mum, but Rosie stamped on her foot.

'Did you say . . . *together*?' said Mum.

'*Together*?' I howled.

'We're soooooo sorrylicious, Mrs G,' said Rosie, ignoring me and fluttering her eyelids. 'If you let us stay with you, I promise we'll have so many more fun times together in the future. And Roman and I will be the best of friends.'

'Do I get any say in this?' I asked, but nobody was listening to me.

Mum clasped her hands together. 'Oh, how romantic. Of course you can stay with us!'

'Did you not *hear* what Rosie's mum said to you?' I said in disbelief.

But Mum didn't listen because Rosie threw her arms round her. 'Thanks, MUM!' she cried. But over Mum's shoulder she was staring at me like a crocodile eyeing up a particularly tasty-looking zebra.

I put my head in my hands. This was a complete and utter disaster.

After she'd let go of my mum, Rosie pulled out her phone and began filming herself. 'Amaze-alicious news, fans. The wedding's back on. Log in tomorrow to see me and my BFF Roman in our special wedding outfits. Mwah.'

'Kill me now,' sighed Rosie's mum, putting on her sunglasses.

'Shush!' snapped Rosie. 'So. All set, then?'

'On one condition,' said Dad. 'I'm choosing the next campsite.'

'No w—' began Rosie's dad but Rosie elbowed him in the ribs. 'Oh. All right then.'

There was an ancient caravanning book in the car. Dad flicked through it and found the closest site to where the wedding was being held.

'It's called Full Moon Caravan Park,' he said, chuffed to be in charge at last. 'It's only an hour from the farm where they're getting married. It'll take us all of today to get there, but then we won't be in a rush before the wedding tomorrow.'

'What facilities has this site got?' asked Rosie's mum. 'Gym? Sauna? Swimming pool?'

Dad squinted at the book. 'No idea. It just says it's "a stripped-back site, as nature intended".'

'Stripped back and as nature intended?' said Rosie's mum. 'Sounds awful.'

'No, it sounds *amazing*,' said Dad. 'Simple and quiet. And cheap. It's probably out in the woods or something.'

'Quality!' exclaimed Gamble. 'We can hunt owls for our dinner.'

'Or maybe just climb a tree,' said Vanya, looking a bit disturbed.

'Urgh. I hate the countryside,' said Rosie's mum. 'They'd better have Wi-Fi or I am literally going to pull out my own lungs.'

The cruel part of me wanted to see what this actually looked like.

'Agreed? Full Moon Caravan Park?' asked Dad.

'S'pose we've got no choice,' said Rosie's mum.

'Hashtag: why not?' said Rosie, forcing a smile. I could tell that she *really* didn't want to stay with us. So why was she pretending she did? It made no sense at all.

'Let's get going!' grinned Dad, who hadn't looked happier since we left home.

'I'll load up the wedding outfits,' said Rosie.

Rosie's dad reversed the little sports car – which miraculously hadn't been damaged in the riot – out of the back of Truckingham Palace.

'Oh,' said Gamble, as we climbed into our car. 'is it OK if we give a lift to The Cheesy Toenails? The person who drives their bus got arrested and they've got a gig tonight.'

'Definitely not!' said everyone at the same time.

Gamble jutted out his bottom lip. 'But I told 'em we would.'

'Well, *un*-tell them,' said Mum. 'The Taylors are already having to abandon their motorhome thanks to you and your band friends.'

Gamble tilted his head to one side, as though he'd just realised something. 'Oh yeah. All right. I'll just let 'em know.'

With that he skipped off to the next field, returning two minutes later with a big smile across his face. If I hadn't been concerned about Rosie, I might have asked him why he was so happy.

Once the route to the Full Moon Caravan Park had been agreed, we set off on the long drive.

Vanya, Gamble and I were squashed in the middle seat of Dad's car, and Rosie's family were following. Luckily, the field had dried out just enough for us to be able to drive across it. The motorhome was left behind to be collected by a recovery company.

Even though I was relieved to be finally getting away from Smash Fest, something was bothering me. Obviously, I was worried about whatever Rosie was planning. And I'm always frightened about what Gamble might do next. But there was more to it than that. I didn't know why, but I had the feeling that where we were heading was even worse than the place we'd just left.

Unfortunately, I would soon be proved correct.

## It's All Down to You

We'd been driving for most of the day when we pulled over at a service station for the loo. There was a massive Squidgy Splodge Doughnut stand, and I was just running out to ask Mum and Dad for some money when I came across Rosie, sitting on her own on a bench. She was talking into her phone.

I tried to go past her, but she grabbed my wrist, while carrying on talking. 'Sorry, Kat,' she said, 'but that's just tough. We ran out of money. We've had to make some changes to your wedding. No. The band have been cancelled. And most of the food. And the flowers. And your dress. Oh. And the tent. So you'll be getting married in your scruffs in a field full of pigs. You can keep the cake though. If you pay for it yourself, of course. Oh, stop crying. It's embarrassing.'

She looked up at me and did a 'boohoo' face.

'Right. Quit blubbing and listen,' she growled into the phone. '*I* have a savings account at the bank with *like* enough money in it to pay for almost everything. So there is a way we can save our big day.'

I didn't like the way she looked at me at this point.

Rosie continued: 'Just tell Roman he needs to do whatever I tell him. If he does, I'll make sure that you have your dream wedding tomorrow. If he doesn't, I'm afraid it'll be a nightmare. '

Rosie held the phone to my ear. Immediately, I was almost deafened by Kat. 'Please, Roman! Do whatever she says! You're the only one who can help. PLEEEAAAAASSSSE!'

This was horrible. What was Rosie planning?

And why was it so important to her? I didn't want to agree to anything, but I couldn't think straight; in my ear, Kat was howling like a stranded sea-cow.

Rosie shrugged at me. 'Up to you, Roman. Save the wedding or ruin her life.'

'Well, OK . . .' I gulped, feeling completely awful. 'As long as it's nothing too bad.'

'The right choice,' grinned Rosie, snatching the phone off me. 'Now, Kat. Sort your life out and turn off the waterworks. If you turn up with red eyes tomorrow you're going to make me look bad.'

Then she hung up and happily skipped off back to her parents' car.

'What was all that about?' asked Vanya, appearing at my shoulder.

'I don't know,' I replied, 'but I think I'll regret it.'

### Full Moon

We got to the Full Moon Caravan Park really late that night. The reception was empty but there was a sign in the window saying that people arriving after ten p.m. should pitch up. Someone would come and collect our money in the morning.

We drove slowly through the darkness, the

caravan bouncing along behind us. There was nobody about. I have to say that the site didn't seem particularly 'stripped back as nature intended' to me. It wasn't out in the woods or the countryside or anything like that – it was just row after row of caravans, motorhomes and tents in a very well-organised field.

Still, I was so worried about Rosie's plans for me that I didn't give this any thought.

Looking back, this was yet another mistake.

We parked up and all squeezed inside the caravan to sleep. All of us except Rosie, that is. First of all she shoved a carrier bag into Mum's arms. 'This is Roman's outfit for tomorrow. I bought it at the shops yesterday, remember. All he has to do is wear it tomorrow and he'll save the wedding.'

'Oooh, how exciting!' exclaimed Mum. 'And will it match yours, Rosie?'

'Sort of,' said Rosie.

I didn't like the way she seemed to be holding back laughter at this point, so I reached for the bag.

'I don't think so, Romy Womy,' said Rosie, playfully slapping my hand. 'You'll spoil the surprise. And don't forget. You promised Kat you'd wear it.'

Then Rosie hauled a massive wheelie suitcase

out of the sports car's boot and began rolling it away.

'Where are you going?' I asked.

Rosie looked at me like I was completely thick. 'To get ready for the wedding, of course.'

'But it's one in the morning,' I said. 'The wedding isn't for ten hours.'

'You're kidding!' she exclaimed. 'I'm gonna have to rush.'

And with that, she whizzed off into the darkness towards the campsite shower block.

'Is she all right going off on her own like that?' said Mum to Rosie's parents.

'Oh yeah,' said Rosie's dad. 'If anyone goes near her make-up we'll hear the screams from miles away.'

'What if she doesn't scream?' said Mum, sounding worried.

Rosie's dad grinned. 'Oh no! Rosie won't be the one screaming. It's the other person we'd be able to hear. She'll stick her make-up pencil in their eyeballs.'

So, minus Rosie, we all traipsed inside the disgusting caravan. And as soon as Rosie's mum had cleaned it from top to toe with antibacterial wipes, we flopped down wherever we could find space.

Everyone else dropped off straight away but I fought against my tiredness for as long as I could. It felt like something awful was brewing, and I was terrified. The sooner I fell asleep, the sooner it would be morning – and the sooner I'd find out what was inside that bag.

# MONDAY

# Rosie Arrives at the Wedding in Style. Sort of

I must've fallen asleep eventually because I opened my eyes to find it was morning. Rosie's mum was sitting at the end of the bench, gripping her knees to her chest and rocking backwards and forwards.

'What are you doing?' I yawned, squirming upright in my sleeping bag. There was a terrible aching fear in my belly, like just before you go on a roller coaster.

The caravan felt cramped with all the people inside it and the windows were completely steamed up. My parents and Rosie's dad were squashed up on the floor, along with me and Vanya. Gamble had felt homesick, so he'd decided to sleep on the toilet.

'We're trapped! Trapped in this dung pit!' howled Rosie's mum. She held a shiny object up in the air and waved it around. 'I tried to escape, but the door handle fell off in my hand!'

She rushed towards the door, treading on Dad's head on the way, and began clawing at the frame with her fingernails.

Suddenly, Rosie burst in, smashing the door into her mum's face and knocking her over. She was wearing the most ridiculous dress I've ever seen. It was a giant white meringue, roughly the size of Wales. She also looked utterly terrified. Her eyes bulged out of her head like she'd just seen a ghost. Or a spider. Or even a ghost spider.

Her dad shot upright. 'What's wrong, cupcake?'

'O-M-W. D-N-G-O-T' she exclaimed, pressing her back up against the door. 'Which is short for: Oh My Word. Do NOT Go Out There!'

Rosie's mum was holding her bleeding nose. 'It can't be worse than in here.'

'What's she on about?' said Dad. He staggered to his feet, opened the kitchen blind and wiped a patch of mist off the little window. Then he peered blearily through it. Immediately his whole body stiffened. 'She's right!'

'What's wrong, Dad?' I asked.

'Someone's stolen the car!' he replied.

Mum shot up next to him, her hand over her mouth. 'Oh gosh! Who would do such a thing?'

'Exactly,' said Rosie's dad, standing behind them and gazing at the empty space next to the caravan. 'Who *would* steal your car? I mean, no offence, but it wasn't exactly worth stealing. It looked like an ice-cream tub on wheels.'

Mum glanced into the bathroom. 'Hang on. Where's Darren?'

'Oh, he escaped hours ago, lucky little maggot,' said Rosie's mum, waving her hand towards Mum. 'I'd have gone with him, but I guessed he was going off to root through the bins or something.'

'And did he take the car?'

Rosie's mum looked confused. 'Course he did. I wasn't going to stop him though, was I? He could've bitten me.'

Dad looked like he was about to say something,

but Rosie interrupted. 'I'm not talking about the car. I'm talking about the . . . the . . . the . . . *people.*'

She had to really spit out the last word, like it was something utterly disgusting.

Mum and Dad squinted out again, and this time they seemed to slowly realise something as well.

Mum's mouth dropped open.

Dad recoiled in horror, covering his eyes.

Rosie's mum fell to her knees.

'I think I might've just burped up some sick,' said Rosie's dad with a painful grimace.

Now, looking back, these reactions all indicated that I definitely **should not** look out of the window. It was pretty obvious that whatever was out there was *not* going to be pleasant.

But there are times when you just can't help yourself. You *have* to look at the scab on your knee, or the mouldy two-week-old sandwich you forgot about in your lunch box, or the collection of head lice that Gamble keeps in that margarine tub.

Unfortunately, *this* was one of those times.

Very slowly, like I was being pulled by a giant

magnet, I found myself standing up, walking over to the main lounge window and wiping away the steam.

## The Worst Caravan Park EVER

**WARNING: Do not read on if you are:**
- very old
- very young
- pregnant
- someone who throws up easily

**If you are any of these things, skip the next few pages. Trust me, this could finish you off.**

Out of the window I could see all the things you'd expect to find in a caravan site: cars, caravans, grass, tents, roads with speed bumps in them, a shower block.

And people.

Loads of normal people doing normal people stuff: reading newspapers and eating breakfast outside their caravans, walking about, riding bikes, chatting with friends, playing swingball, doing yoga stretches on the grass.

But there was one thing about these people that *definitely* was not normal.

Every single one of them was . . . you know . . . I'd rather not say . . . well . . . they were . . . ahem . . . **nude.**

As in wearing no clothes.

As in naked, starkers, in the buff, shirtless, trouserless, UNDERPANTSLESS.

As in utterly revolting. Everywhere you looked, you were staring at skin and . . . other bits.

There were young people. Old people. *Really* old people. Hairy people. Wobbly people. Skinny people. Saggy people. Wrinkly people. Tall people. Short people. Men. Women. People who could've been either. And every single one of them was as bare as the day they were born.

I staggered back across the room and turned away, but then I could see them out of the kitchen window as well. They were swarming everywhere, like gigantic nudey ants.

I closed my eyes, but the image of the naked people was burned into them.

'Where have you brought us, you sicko?' howled Rosie's mum.

'How was I supposed to . . .' began Dad. But

then he realised something. 'Oh no! The caravan site guide!'

Suddenly it all clicked into place: *Full Moon* Caravan Park. A *stripped-back* site. *As nature intended.*

It might as well have said: 'Watch out: bums and boobs everywhere.'

'We need to get out of here,' I said.

'Pronto,' gulped Vanya.

'But we haven't got a door handle,' said Rosie's mum.

'Or a car,' Dad said.

'Or Darren,' added Mum.

We were trapped! What if we had to stay here, unable to leave the caravan? How long before we began to starve? Who would get eaten first? *Huh*, I thought. *Probably me. It's always me.*

'Daddy,' said Rosie, 'if we ever get out of here, you are paying for me to have my memory erased.'

For once, I could completely see where she was coming from. This place was awful. It was like being the only survivors of a zombie apocalypse. Except they weren't zombies who wanted to eat your brains – they wanted to eat your clothes.

There was a sudden knock at the door.

'Don't answer it!' said Mum.

Through the frosted glass, we could see the blurred pink outline of a short, silver-haired man – completely nude. 'Morning all!' came a cheerful voice.

'We're not in,' said Dad. Mum rolled her eyes at him.

'If you stay still they can't see you,' I whispered.

'I think that's dinosaurs, not nudists,' said Vanya.

'Get lost, you naked monstrosity!' cried Rosie.

Although this was quite harsh, I have to say I sort of agreed with her again.

'I've come to collect your site fees,' said the voice, not so cheerful now. 'You owe eighteen pounds.'

'We can't,' said Mum. 'Our door handle's broken in here. It only opens from the outside.'

This was a mistake.

'Oh, you poor people,' said the man. 'Allow me.'

He opened the door and just stood there in front of us like it was the most natural thing in the world! Honestly! What could be *less* natural than being in the nude? It was horrible.

Someone screamed, and I realised it was me.

Rosie's dad grabbed a twenty-pound note out of Dad's wallet. Then he threw the money out of the door and slammed it shut so hard that it bounced open again.

The man was still there, and still totally naked. He bent over to pick up the twenty pounds, which was easily the most disgusting thing I've ever seen.

'That is going to give me nightmares for the rest of my life,' said Rosie.

'I'll have to come back with your two pounds change,' said the man, standing up. 'I don't have pockets.'

'Keep it!' Rosie's dad said.

The man waddled away, shaking his head like *we* were the weirdoes.

Mum clapped her hands together. 'Right. We need to find Darren, get the car and get out of here.'

'N-O-P,' said Rosie's mum, grabbing her husband's hand and pulling him towards the door. 'Not Our Problem. Your car. Your strange little friend. We're leaving.'

'Amen to that,' said Rosie's dad. 'Come on, Rosie.'

'But what about us?' asked Mum. 'And the wedding?'

Rosie stepped forward. 'Don't worry. The wedding can't start without Roman. The whole thing depends on him. Your car will turn up, I'm sure of it. Just make sure Roman is in his outfit.'

Before Mum could answer, they'd gone.

'Right,' sighed Dad as their car disappeared. 'One of us needs to go out and look for Darren.'

For a long time, we all looked at each other.

Then a car horn beeped outside.

## A Quick Escape

Gamble jogged into the caravan, the car engine still running outside. 'Let's get going, innit.'

'Where have you been?' asked Dad. 'And why did you steal my car?'

Gamble picked a zit on the back of his scalp then ate the crusty scab off the top off it. 'Didn't nick it. *Borrowed* it. Woke up early and wanted to check out all the nudies and that. It was well good. You should've seen this old geezer round by the shop. He had a proper mad birthmark on his w—'

'Darren!' interrupted Mum. 'What you did was illegal.'

'Eh?' said Gamble angrily. 'So now it's against the law for kids to nick cars and drive 'em about, is it?'

'Well . . . yes,' replied Mum.

'Really?' said Gamble, surprised. 'Since when?'

Vanya frowned. 'Since . . . er . . . *always*.'

Gamble sniffed. 'Learn something new every day, innit. Anyway. Doesn't matter cos I brought it back, but like I said let's do one.'

He was hopping around shiftily and continually peeking out of the windows. The last time I saw him this agitated was that time at school when those Foundation Stage kids went missing and it turned out he'd tried to bury them in a time capsule.

'Are you all right?' I said to him. 'You're . . . sweating.'

Gamble wiped his underarms on the curtains, which is one of the few things on earth that could've made them smell worse than they already did. 'Just a bit hot.'

'Whatever's happened, we've got a wedding to get to,' sighed Mum.

This was the best news I'd heard all morning. It took less than two minutes for Dad to attach the caravan to the tow bar and for us to bundle into the car. Before we knew it, we were driving off.

Vanya and I were looking down at the floor of the car so we couldn't see the nudists. Gamble had insisted on climbing into the boot, folding up one of the back seats and sitting alone, with all the bags piled up around him.

We'd been driving slowly for about two minutes when Dad slammed on the brakes. 'What do *they* want?'

Without thinking, I glanced up and **urgh**! It was horrible! Off to our right, a whole family of nudists – a woman, two kids a few years younger than me, and (worst of all) a grandma – were pointing towards us and waving their hands (as well as everything else).

'They don't look very happy,' said Dad, as the family started trotting towards us.

'Maybe they don't like people wearing clothes,' suggested Vanya.

The people were getting closer. 'Should we find out what they want?' asked Mum.

This seemed like a bad idea. The people had broken into a sprint. It was horrible. *Everything* was bouncing around as they ran. Within two seconds, they'd reached the car and were bashing on the windows with their palms. It was as if we'd driven into the world's most disgusting safari park.

'DRIVE!' yelled Gamble from the back.

Dad didn't need asking twice. He slammed his foot down. The tyres squealed, the car lurched forward, and within seconds we were out on the open road, with the nudists behind us, waving their fists.

'What was all that about?' asked Dad.

'Nothing to do with me,' replied Gamble.

I turned round to look at him and he growled back at me. Something very strange was going on.

## Everything REALLY Starts to Go Wrong

We drove for about twenty minutes, then stopped at a roadside café for breakfast and to get changed for the wedding.

Gamble refused to get out of the car. At the time, I was happy about this. He has absolutely no table manners. His party trick during school dinners is to stuff his nostrils with heavily peppered mashed potato, then see how far he can sneeze it out.

Still, the fact that he was turning down free food should've been yet another clue that something wasn't right.

Unfortunately, we were all so hungry that we ignored it. *And* we ignored the way that he wouldn't let us open the boot. *And* how he insisted on passing Mum her suitcase, the bag with my outfit in it and Vanya's rucksack over the top of the middle seats instead of letting us get them ourselves. *And,* for that matter, how he'd spread coats over the rest of the bags while we were driving.

Now, looking back, it seems obvious what was happening. But when you're starving hungry and standing outside a café called Sue Ellen's American Diner – Home of the Breakfast Doughnut, you don't really notice the little things, even if they're staring you in the face.

Anyway, I had other things to worry about first.

You see, after we'd wolfed down our grub (I'd never had a bacon and egg doughnut before, but I had four for my main course and a jam one for dessert) we went to the loo to get ready for the wedding.

And that's when everything REALLY started to go wrong.

'I'm not wearing it!' I said, stamping my feet. 'I'll look ridiculous.'

Mum held up my outfit. 'Oh, don't be a baby.'

'But I'm going to be DRESSED like a baby!' I snapped.

I was, as well.

Inside the bag Rosie had given us, we'd found the following items:

- one blonde curly wig
- one toy bow and arrow
- one giant nappy.

Yes. That's right. Rosie was going to make me stand in front of two hundred people while dressed in a nappy.

This was terrible.

'You're not going to be any old baby!' said Mum. 'You'll be Cupid – the angel of love.'

'And that's meant to make me feel bet—'

I was interrupted by Mum's phone ringing. 'Ooh. It's Lee. I wonder what he wants on his wedding day,' she said, before answering. 'Hello, Lee. Are you OK? Yes of course. Here he is.'

She passed the phone over to me.

'Roman,' said my cousin Lee. He sounded seriously panicked. 'I've just had a text from Rosie. Are you wearing the outfit?'

'No. And I'm not going to either.'

'But you have to! Please!' he begged. 'The

wedding's supposed to be in two hours but the tent's not been put up yet. The food's not been cooked. There are no flowers. Kat's dress hasn't been delivered. The woman who's doing the service hasn't even turned up. Rosie's told them all they can't do anything until you're in costume.'

My blood went cold.

'What's going on?' asked Mum.

'You can't tell her anything!' said Lee. 'Rosie says that the wedding's off if your mum finds out that you're being forced to dress up.'

In the background I could hear Kat screaming hysterically. 'It's ruined! Ruined!'

'Please, Roman. Only you can save it!' said Lee.

I took a deep breath. What else could I do? 'OK,' I said finally, my mouth dry.

'Brilliant! He's going to wear it!' cried Lee.

Kat came on the phone. I could barely hear her through the tears and snot. 'Thank you so much, Roman. Thank you. See you soon.'

She hung up. 'Could this day get any worse?' I asked.

Answer: *yes. Of course it could.*

As Mum passed me the bag, a piece of paper fell

out of it and she picked it up. 'Oooh, look. Instructions from Rosie.'

'Great.'

'It says here you have to skip into the ceremony, dropping rose petals onto the ground. Then you've got to do a special "lovey-dovey" dance in front of everyone. Then you've got to shoot yourself in the head with your bow and arrow.'

I felt like doing the last bit right now.

'How romantic . . .' said Mum dreamily. 'Just think. If you do this little favour for Rosie, she might even agree to be your girlfriend.'

This didn't even deserve a reply. I ground my teeth together and put on the stupid outfit.

Vanya is a good friend – when she saw me in the nappy outside the toilet she only laughed for about three minutes. But, back at the car, there was another hint that something wasn't right with Gamble. He didn't laugh at me at all. In fact, he was looking seriously anxious about something, and wouldn't even eat the extra doughnut we'd brought him.

'Right!' said Dad. 'Let's get moving. We should be there with a good hour to spare.'

He hadn't thought about the traffic though. We'd

only been driving for about five minutes when we slowed down into a long queue.

'Oh great,' he said. 'Roadworks. Or someone's broken down. Not to worry. Plenty of time to get there.'

I forced a smile at this last bit. I was kind of hoping that we might be so late we'd miss it altogether. This made me feel bad though. I mean, if I didn't show up, would Rosie honestly cancel the wedding? You couldn't put anything past her.

The traffic barely moved for about forty minutes. All the time, Mum and Dad were getting more concerned about being late, I was getting more *hopeful* about being late, and Gamble was getting more and more twitchy in the back, looking over his shoulder as though he was worried he was being followed.

Sadly, the traffic eventually melted away and we began moving again.

'Phew!' exclaimed Mum, looking at the map. 'If we have a clear run from here we'll arrive just in time.'

This turned out to be a bit optimistic.

We'd been cruising along the road for about five minutes when we heard it for the first time.

*THUD!*

It came from behind.

'Did something fall off the caravan?' said Dad, peering in the rear-view mirror.

'Don't ask me,' said Gamble. Then he sniffed. 'Does your boot open from the inside?'

'Why would you need to know that?' I asked.

Gamble shrugged.

Then, a minute later, *THUD!* Again.

'I think it's *inside*,' said Mum, turning round. 'Is there something wrong back there, Darren?'

'Why's everyone having a go at me I ain't done nothing leave me alone,' wailed Darren. He's always overreacting like this, by the way. One time at school, his teaching assistant Miss Clegg asked him to stop swinging on his chair, so he ran out of the classroom to the staff car park and wiped his bare bottom across her windscreen.

There was a long silence, then a load of restless rustling from Gamble.

'Are you OK?' I asked.

'Yep,' said Gamble, punching the pile of coats.

Ordinarily, this wouldn't have surprised me. Gamble is always lashing out at inanimate objects. Like when he kicked a tree because it 'thought it was hard'. But, this time, something very strange happened.

The pile of coats *moaned* when he hit it.

'Shut up!' hissed Gamble, punching the pile of coats again.

'What's going on?' I asked.

'I always fight myself when I'm bored,' replied Gamble, trying to look innocent.

And then it emerged from under the coats.

A head.

Nothing else. Poking out of the coats. Old man. Grey hair matted with dried blood. Big bruise like an egg above one of his goggly eyes. Mouth hanging open in confusion or . . . *death*?

It groaned.

I screamed.

'What the?' exclaimed Dad, swerving the car across two lanes.

But this wasn't all.

I mean, it was bad enough when I thought it might have just been a head without a body attached. But things were about to get a lot worse.

The coats moved, revealing the rest of the person as he tried to scramble towards me.

He was fully alive.

And, worse than that, *he was fully naked*.

'There's a nude old man in our car!' I howled.

Everyone fell into a mad panic. Mum and Vanya were squealing. Dad was flinging the steering wheel around, trying to get the car under control. I was pushing the naked old man off my head as he slithered over the back of the seats to get away from Gamble, who was hitting him with a shoe. It was total chaos.

'Pull over!' yelled Mum.

Dad slammed on the brakes, steering wildly in front of a lorry before screeching to a halt in a lay-by. The old man flew forward, landing upside down with his head in Mum's lap and his . . . *other bits* a lot closer to my face than I liked.

There were a few moments when everyone sat there, shocked. Then Vanya broke the silence.

'Isn't that Rosie and her family?' she asked.

## Burn Rubber

'The last thing I remember,' said the naked man, rubbing the lump on his head, 'I was crossing the road at the caravan site. Then everything went black.'

He was sitting in the doorway of the caravan,

his ankle dangling off at an awkward angle. Thankfully, he now had Dad's coat wrapped around his waist. Mum was busy rummaging around in the car, trying to find a first-aid kit.

'He just stepped out in front of me when I was driving,' said Gamble, leaning out of the car boot. 'What was I supposed to do, *not* run him over?'

'That's kind of the idea,' said Dad.

'Well, you definitely weren't looking where you were going,' said the man.

'Course I wasn't looking,' said Gamble, as if this should've been obvious. 'I had nudey women to check out, innit.'

'But how did he end up in my boot?' said Dad, confused.

'I didn't wanna get busted, so I chucked him in when he was out cold,' said Gamble. 'I'm proper strong, me. Thought I might be able to throw him out of the boot while we were driving along.'

'Thanks a bunch,' said the naked man.

'That wouldn't have happened,' said Dad, trying to reassure him.

I wasn't so sure.

'And anyway, why *was* a child driving your car?' said the naked man to Dad.

'Yeah!' said Gamble. 'Answer me that, Roman's dad.'

Unbelievable! He was trying to make out that it was Dad's fault.

Just then, Rosie and her family strutted over. Her mum was wearing a hideous floral dress with what looked like half an emu strapped to her head.

'What is *that*?' she said, pointing at the old man.

'It's a *he*,' said Vanya.

'Whatever,' said Rosie. 'Ditch him. We all need to get in your car and get moving.'

'Eh?' asked Dad.

'Spot of bother with our car,' replied Rosie's dad, a bit embarrassed. 'Rosie was trying to dry her fingernails out of the window as I was driving and she accidentally dropped her nail varnish. We had to stop all the traffic and get it back.'

'Wait a second,' I said, 'you caused that traffic jam? Just so you could get your nail varnish back?'

Rosie stared at me like I was completely dim. 'Of course. I'd only done one hand, and Rosie Taylor is not turning up at a wedding with different coloured nails. This is going out live on Rosie-dot-TV.'

'I'm not going to film it,' muttered Vanya.

'Fine. I'll do it on a selfie stick,' said Rosie. 'And

may I say, Roman, you look perfect. The whole world is going to laugh at you. I mean love you.'

I grunted at her.

'Daddy was so sweet,' Rosie continued. 'He had to park his car right across both lanes of the road to stop everyone. He was crawling around on the tarmac looking for it for ages.'

'What if there had been an emergency?' asked Vanya. 'You could've blocked an ambulance or a fire engine.'

Rosie rolled her eyes. 'Oh pur-lease. I'm a global internet celebrity. I think my nails are a little bit more important than some ordinary person's life.'

'Anyway,' said her dad, taking up the story, 'then some idiot bashed the side of the car trying to squeeze past and now the wheels won't turn properly. So we were wondering . . .'

They all looked hopefully at my parents.

'Well,' said Dad, 'we're actually worried about what we can do with this gentleman.'

Rosie tutted. 'Who, like, gives a monkey's undies? Dump him here and let's get to this wedding.'

'Great point,' said Rosie's mum. 'We're going to be *sooooo* late if we're not careful. It starts in twenty minutes.'

'You can't leave me here,' said the naked man. 'I don't have any money. Or a phone. Or any clothes. What do you want me to do?'

Rosie shrugged. 'DKDCL. Don't Know Don't Care, Loser. Live out here in the wild and eat squirrels or something.'

The man's mouth opened and closed a few times.

At that point, Mum came back, holding a bandage and a bottle of TCP. 'Oh, hello, Rosie. Doesn't she look gorgeous, Roman?'

I said nothing, but Rosie instantly flicked back to nice mode. 'Really? You're so kind. Daddy had an ickle accident. Please could you give us a lift to the wedding?'

Mum sighed. 'Oh, I'm so sorry but I think we need to get this gentleman to hospital. He might have concussion.'

'But. But. What about the wedding?' asked Rosie. 'I *need* to be at that wedding. And so does Roman.'

I noticed her slug's bum mouth getting tight again. Blotches were appearing on her forehead.

'I'm sure they'll understand,' said Mum. 'And anyway, we'll be there in time for the cake. Roman, Vanya, hop into the car. Dad and I will help the gentleman.'

Vanya and I did as we were told. The boot was still open, so we could hear the conversation outside.

Rosie's mum tutted loudly. 'So, you're telling me that this man's health is more important than us getting to this wedding on time?'

'Er . . . yes?' offered Mum. 'We'd love to give you a lift but he *needs* to see a doctor. There's a bus stop in the lay-by. Maybe you could catch a bus to the wedding?'

'A bus?!' howled Rosie's mum, as if she'd just been asked to ride on the back of a giant rat. 'Taylors do *not* catch buses. We're not tramps.'

'Daddy! Do Something!' cried Rosie, forgetting that she was meant to seem nice in front of my mum. 'If I'm late for this wedding I will literally buy a nuclear bomb and blow up everyone in the world.'

'Cool,' said Gamble, for some reason.

Then Rosie's dad did something terrible. Before anyone could stop him, he'd darted to our car and jumped in through the driver's door. 'Let's move!'

The engine roared into life. Rosie's mum leapt into the passenger seat and Rosie threw herself into the boot next to Gamble.

'What are you doing?' said Dad, frozen in the lay-by.

'Making sure my daughter gets to this wedding on time!'

'But . . .'

'Burn rubber!' screamed Rosie, yanking down the boot.

The car jolted forward. Out of the back window, I could see the naked man clinging on to the doorway of the caravan as it bounced behind us. He hopped along the tarmac a couple of times – losing Dad's coat in the process – before falling inside. For a few moments, his bare legs and backside were dangling out of the doorway. Then he hauled himself in and the door slammed shut behind him.

'What about Mum and Dad?' I said, panicking.

They were still standing there in the lay-by, staring open-mouthed as we screeched back onto the road.

'Maybe *they* can get a bus,' said Rosie's mum icily.

Within ten seconds, we were hurtling along at ninety-eight miles an hour, so fast that I was pinned back in my seat and feeling slightly sick. The engine of Dad's old car was screaming like an animal in pain and, behind us, the caravan was swinging around all over the place. Mum and Dad could no longer be seen.

'Forget them, Roman,' said Rosie from behind me. She was attempting to add the finishing touches to her make-up in front of a tiny handheld mirror. 'We don't need your ugly mother and her cheap clothes. She'll only ruin the wedding.'

'Don't be horrible about my mum!' I said, turning round. 'You've been sucking up to her all weekend.'

Rosie snorted. 'Of course I have. I had to be nice to her, otherwise I wouldn't have got her to do what I wanted.'

'And what was that?' I asked, even though I already knew the answer.

'Making you look like a complete idiot on the internet, of course,' she said. 'It's been my plan from the start. The moment you came to our house, I could see how impressed your mother was. She got all giddy and excited about our money. I knew straight away I could get her to do anything I wanted. All I had to do was dangle the carrot of friendship in front of her. Good grief – as if we'd ever *choose* to spend time with people as frightful and poor as you.'

'She's right,' said Rosie's mum to herself. 'Ghastly woman. Sorry. Did I say that out loud? Whoops.'

'But, you know,' continued Rosie, 'I have to say I *liked* spending time with your family. It's nice to know how pov-tabulous tramps live. It's a bit like visiting a zoo and looking at the giant beetles. You know – they might be disgusting, brainless and gross. But you have to admit, they *are* fascinating.'

My hands tightly gripped the toy bow and arrow. 'Pull over,' I said, as the speedometer crept past a hundred and ten. 'I'm not going to this wedding and I'm taking off this stupid outfit.'

'Not so fast,' said Rosie, finally looking up from the mirror. 'You so much as touch that nappy and the wedding's over. You'll ruin everyone's day *and* Kat's life. You wouldn't want that on your conscience, would you?'

I grunted under my breath.

Rosie gave a hideous smile. 'I thought not. Finally, I'll be able to get my own back on you *and* make the world love me again, all in one day. I've got half a million subscribers now, you know. Including all the people from school. And they're all going to watch me dominate this wedding *and* see you dressed like that! Imagine: the whole planet will be loving me and laughing at you at the same time. Finally, hashtag Rosie Taylor will be back!'

She cackled like an evil drain.

'You're a really nasty person,' said Vanya to Rosie.

'I try my best,' said Rosie, like this was a compliment.

'That's my girl,' said Rosie's dad proudly.

## Red Lights Don't Stop Us

We carried on speeding along the road. I was sitting there, feeling ill and seriously angry at the same time. Gamble, on the other hand, was enjoying himself a bit too much in the back seat. 'Faster! Faster!' he yelled, winding down his window and leaning out.

'Where are you going?' I said.

He gripped the frame to pull himself out. 'I'm gonna surf on the roof!'

'Get back inside!' I yelled. 'You'll be turned into scrambled eggs.'

'OMG! Just let him go,' said Rosie matter-of-factly. She'd gone back to doing her make-up. 'He'll probably be fine. Hey, Vanya – get my phone and film me. My followers need an update on how gorgeous I look.'

'Drop dead,' said Vanya.

Unfortunately, Rosie didn't have time to do this because Gamble, who was now halfway out of the window, suddenly noticed something.

'Hey, look!' he called. 'There's a police car behind us!'

*Oh great.*

Rosie's dad looked in the wing mirror. 'So they wanna play catch, do they? They're not spoiling my daughter's big day.'

The police car was gaining on us. It pulled alongside and the policeman in the passenger seat pointed towards the side of the road. Gamble turned himself round and pulled a moony, his bare bottom hanging out of the window. This was not a clever idea. The police car immediately started flashing its lights.

We were just passing a junction. Without warning, Rosie's dad flung the car onto the side road. The wheels skidded and squealed as the car spun sideways. Behind us, the caravan swung round like the flicking tail of a snake. The terrified face of the naked man was pressed against its front window as it rose up on two wheels, then slammed down again. Everyone screamed, apart from Gamble, who was laughing like a maniac.

With no time to turn behind us, the police car carried on along the main road. Mr Taylor slapped the steering wheel. 'See you, coppers! Five minutes and we'll be there.'

'Daddy, what have you done to my face?' howled Rosie. Her lipstick had drawn an ugly red line across her cheek. She looked terrible, which made me feel a little better. Maybe she wouldn't want to go to the wedding any more.

Rosie's mum turned round in her seat. 'OMG, darling!' she said. 'You look like that American singer Lady Goo Goo. She did something similar for that concert, remember?'

'Oh yeah!' said Rosie, admiring herself in the mirror. 'I *do* look amazing. Everyone will be looking at me! I'll totally steal the show.'

'Oh no,' said Mr Taylor.

The police car had reappeared behind and was gaining on us. Ahead, the road crossed a railway at a level crossing. Rosie's dad glared into the rear-view mirror. 'The farm's just over the tracks and up that hill. Look – I can see the marquee. Hold on, people. We can make it!'

The engine squealed as the car surged even faster.

But there was a problem.

Right then, the lights of the level crossing began to flash. The gates began to lower. There was a train coming!

'Speed up, Daddy!' Rosie yelled.

'Slow down, you lunatic!' I cried.

'We can make it!' Rosie's dad growled. 'Red lights can't stop us!'

Ahead of us, the level crossing gates were halfway down. Everyone screwed up their faces and gripped their seats. Behind us in the caravan, the naked man was clinging to the window frame for dear life.

THUD!

The car hit a little ramp and flew through the air, the roof skimming under the bottom of the gate.

Then we landed and

*KERCHUNK!*

The car stopped dead.

I flew forward, the seatbelt slicing painfully into my shoulders. A moment later, Gamble shot through the air over my head and smashed face first into the back of Mr Taylor's seat.

'That was proper mental!' he said groggily.

Next to me, Vanya was gripping hold of her door handle with one hand and patting her heart with the other. Behind, the crash had caused Rosie to headbutt her entire make-up bag, the contents of which were smeared across her face. She looked like a really terrifying clown.

'All alive?' asked Rosie's dad. 'Great! Let's get moving.'

He revved the engine but nothing happened.

We were stuck.

*What was going on?*

I looked out of the back window and gulped. I couldn't believe it. The bottom of the gate had pierced the flimsy roof of the caravan like a giant can opener, and was now pinning the caravan to the ground. And, because we were attached to it, we couldn't move.

But that wasn't the worst thing.

Most of the caravan was sticking out across the train tracks. And the train was getting closer. This was serious.

Inside the caravan, we could see the naked man slapping desperately on the window. He disappeared to open the door but of course there was no handle. He reappeared at the window again, his face twisted with fear.

Rosie's dad revved the engine a second time.

Again, we didn't move. On the other side of the track, the policemen were out of their car, looking on helplessly.

'Wooohooo!' cheered Gamble. 'Here comes the train!'

It was thundering along the tracks towards the caravan, horn blasting. There was no way it could stop in time.

'Someone help him!' cried Vanya.

'Someone get me some wet wipes for my face!' cried Rosie.

Vanya and I scrabbled to open the car doors.

We were too late.

There was a roar of wheels. A terrible screech of brakes. But the train was never going to stop. I couldn't look; my hand was frozen on the door handle. The car engine continued to rev. Mr Taylor swore loudly. And then . . .

There was a deafening explosion as the train ploughed through the caravan. I turned around to see metal and plastic exploding into the air like a huge caravan volcano.

No longer trapped, the car suddenly shot forward. We surged away from the level crossing, dragging the remaining half of the caravan behind us, and crashed straight through a hedge and into a field.

The car skidded to a halt, its engine steaming. Up ahead, a hundred pigs stared at us quizzically. But there was only one thing on my mind.

'What about the man in the caravan?' I said.

'What about my face?' cried Rosie.

Her dad had already jumped out of the car to see what was happening behind.

'Hurry up, Daddy, you complete snail's nipple!' yelled Rosie. 'We're a minute late!'

Vanya was just about to punch her. But then we saw him – the naked man. He was still standing there, next to the window, on the last remaining few centimetres of caravan floor. His face was frozen in terror and he was clutching onto the curtains.

'He's alive!' I yelled.

The long train had finally ground to a halt on the line, so the policemen still weren't able to get past, but above us a helicopter was circling the field.

'Let's help him,' I said.

But I didn't get the chance.

The car lurched forward again. I spun round.

In the confusion, Rosie had managed to crawl over the seats without me noticing. She was now in the driving seat, and suddenly we were racing up the hill, the engine screaming. 'Out of the way, pigs!' she screamed, smashing through a pig shelter and sending the poor animals running for their lives.

Behind us, the naked man was holding onto the curtains for dear life. He was being dragged on his belly across the field, spinning over and over through the mud and filth.

'Can I have a go after him?' asked Gamble.

'Which pedal's the brake?' shouted Rosie.

She didn't find it though because the car charged forward even faster. And then we burst through the gate at the top of the field and the marquee was right in front of us.

For an instant, everything went white.

Then we were *inside* the wedding, crashing straight along the aisle. People dived out of our way. Chairs exploded into splinters.

And finally, with half of the marquee and the naked man still attached to the back of the car, we skidded to a halt millimetres away from Lee and Kat.

## Grand Entrance

I'm not an expert but there are probably rules for how you should arrive at a wedding. You should be early. And quiet. And not draw attention to yourself. And be on your best behaviour. And definitely *don't* break anything.

What you probably *shouldn't* do is arrive late in a stolen car, crashing through the side of the marquee and causing half of it to collapse. You probably shouldn't be dressed in a giant nappy. You definitely shouldn't bring a kid like Gamble along. You really shouldn't destroy the band's instruments, or nearly crush the bride and groom. And, under no circumstances, should you be dragging a naked old man along the ground behind you, holding on to the back of an exploded caravan.

Lee's mouth was wide open in a perfect O. Kat was on her knees, crying. One hundred and fifty people were staring at us, stunned. The members of the band were examining a smashed violin and a very flat trombone.

I felt awful.

'You'd better not have started yet!' snapped

Rosie, storming out of the car. 'I've not even sung, and I haven't set up the webcam.'

Lee didn't seem to know what to say to this. But in any case, he didn't have the chance to answer because, at that moment, the naked man limped over and grabbed him by the lapels. 'Save me from them!' he begged. 'They're all nutters.'

My auntie Susan – Lee's mum – fainted on the spot.

Vanya, Gamble and I were watching all of this from the car. And things were getting more and more serious by the moment.

'There they are!' came a voice from behind us. Through the crumpled material of the marquee ran four police officers and the naked man's family (all of whom were still completely nude). When they saw they were in a wedding though, they kind of froze, unsure what to do next.

Worst of all though, Rosie had pulled her selfie stick out and was murdering some awful tune about wanting to marry herself cos no man would ever be good enough.

Gamble snorted back some snot and spat out of the window. 'This wedding's rubbish, there hasn't even been a fight yet.'

'Look at that poor woman's face,' said Vanya, nodding towards Kat.

For a moment, my eyes met Kat's. She looked terrible. I hadn't seen anyone so upset since the time when Gamble's air rifle got confiscated by the head teacher.

'We'd better get out,' I sighed, and I climbed out of the car.

Immediately, everyone turned towards me.

'What is *that*!' cried one of the guests.

'Who invited the baby?' said someone else.

'Do you need someone to change your nappy?'

A couple of people laughed bitterly.

'Leave him alone!' said Vanya. 'He's obviously Cupid, the angel of love.'

Someone said, 'Awwww,' like I was a half-crippled kitten.

And at that moment, it all became too much for Kat. 'It's RUINED!' she wailed. 'My whole wedding is RUINED!'

I really didn't know what to say.

Rosie did though. 'Kat. Will you shut up? I'm trying to sing my special song here.'

The guests gasped.

I looked from Kat to Rosie and back to Kat

again. Then I looked at my hands. I was still holding the toy bow and arrow. Without thinking, I lifted it up and fired.

A hundred and fifty pairs of eyes followed the arrow as it arced beautifully through the air and, amazingly, hit Rosie right in the middle of the forehead.

Some people in the crowd laughed.

'Nice shot!' said someone.

Rosie glared at me, her mouth opening and closing in shock. The sucker was stuck to her skin. She looked like a really low-budget Dalek. 'I'll get you for this!'

But I didn't care, because Kat wasn't crying any more. In fact, the tiniest hint of a smile had appeared in the corner of her mouth.

Her words from earlier came back to me. *Only you can save the wedding, Roman.*

I realised that people were staring at me, like they were waiting for something else. The arrow had been good but it wouldn't be enough. The wedding was still in the balance. Kat's head tilted to one side. My auntie woke up and groggily got to her feet. At the back of the tent, my parents had somehow arrived and were standing watching.

Vanya squeezed my hand. 'You can do it, Roman.'

And before I knew it, words were tumbling out of my mouth. 'Er. I didn't want to dress like this. But I am Cupid. The angel of love. And weddings are meant to be about love. So why don't . . . er . . . Lee and Kat just get married because . . .' My belly was flipping over and over. 'They . . . love each other and that would be nice. And I didn't want to ruin your day. And I'm sorry about the tent.'

Incredibly, this seemed to stop everyone from being angry. A few people even cheered.

'That fat baby's got a point,' said someone.

'*Fat?*' I said. 'Steady on.'

And Lee pulled Kat to her feet.

This would've been quite a nice moment, but Rosie grabbed him by his sleeve. 'Stop it. You can't get married yet. I've not even finished my song and – YYYYOOOOOOOOWWWWWW!'

At that exact moment, a pig burst into the marquee and flipped her up onto its back. Then she rode it backwards around and around the marquee three times before it dumped her head first into the wedding cake.

The guests applauded enthusiastically.

'Time to get married,' said my cousin Lee. Then he did something disgusting. He kissed Kat right on the lips.

And everybody cheered as eighty million bacteria swam between their mouths.

Yuck!

# Epilogue

So I guess the wedding wasn't a complete disaster in the end.

Once they'd fixed up the marquee.

And got rid of the pigs.

And found some clothes for the naked family.

And persuaded the police not to arrest anyone.

Of course, it was really boring, and I was forced to keep my ridiculous outfit on the whole time. But it wasn't as bad as it could've been.

For a start, Rosie had been so humiliated that she couldn't bear to stay. Unfortunately, her parents still had no money, so they had to take a hat round the guests and beg for enough cash to get them home. Everyone was so glad to see the back of them that they soon had enough.

Seeing them snivelling around like this made Mum actually feel sorry for them. And it made her admit that she'd been a total nightmare all weekend. She even apologised for everything: for losing her brain just because the Taylors were rich; for dragging us off on holiday with them in the first place; for getting carried away trying to impress them. And, most of all, for thinking that Rosie and I could EVER be boyfriend and girlfriend.

There was only one problem. Rosie had crushed the band's instruments. There was no music at all, and after a while everyone was getting a little bit bored.

But then Gamble made a phone call.

Half an hour later, The Cheesy Toenails rocked up in their brand new tour bus, which used to be Truckingham Palace. Gamble had saved it from the scrap heap by giving them the keys just before we left Smash Fest. And it turned out they weren't just a thrash metal band either. They actually played some nice, quiet music for people to boogie along to.

Even I had a dance with Vanya, although Gamble

got in a sulk because the Toenails weren't allowed to play their 'awesomest' tune – 'Blood-soaked Wedding Massacre'.

Best of all though, at least half the wedding cake was saved. And that wasn't all. First of all, it wasn't just fruit cake – there was a whole layer of chocolate cake as well. But even better than that, nobody else wanted any after the pigs had been near it. I ended up eating about three times my own body weight.

Result!

So all in all, if you forgot about the awful weekend, and the terrible outfit, and the fact that I almost lost my best friend, the wedding wasn't all that bad after all.

Sort of.

But that doesn't mean I ever want to go to another one ever, ever again.

MARK LOWERY grew up in Preston but now lives near Cambridge with his young family. Some of the time he is a primary-school teacher. In the olden days he used to spend his time doing lots of active stuff like running, hiking, snowboarding and swimming, but now he prefers staying in and attempting to entertain his children. He plays the guitar badly and speaks appalling Italian but he knows a lot about biscuits. In his mind he is one of the great footballers of his generation, although he is yet to demonstrate this on an actual football pitch. He has an MA in Writing for Children and his first two books – *Socks Are Not Enough* and *Pants Are Everything* – were both shortlisted for the Roald Dahl Funny Prize. Mark is also the author of the Roman Garstang series (*The Jam Doughnut that Ruined my Life*; *The Chicken Nugget Ambush*; *The Attack of the Woolly Jumper*; *The Great Caravan Catastrophe*). He is yet to find a cake that he doesn't like. Follow Mark on www.marklowery.co.uk or on Twitter: @hellomarklowery

# Piccadilly
## PRESS

Thank you for choosing a Piccadilly Press book.

If you would like to know more about our authors, our books or if you'd just like to know what we're up to, you can find us online.

## www.piccadillypress.co.uk

You can also find us on:

## We hope to see you soon!